THE
ENDLESS DREAM

ISBN: 978-1-936955-26-8

Second Edition

Typesetting by Nathaniel Kennon Perkins

Front Cover: Melancholy and Mystery of a Street (Giorgio de Chirico, 1914)

Back Cover: The Joys and Enigmas of a Strange Hour (Giorgio de Chirico, 1913)

Published by Bäuu Press
Golden, CO
www.bauuinstitute.com

THE
ENDLESS DREAM:

a destiny

by Anonymous
edited by Wayne Omura

Bäuu Press
Golden, CO

To the memory of the first and last expedition.

Zero point nine nine nine extended equals one.

No one knows me, for I am not real. I am an illusion that deceives the eyes. I am an illusion that distorts the mind. All who think they know me, know only an illusion, for the real me is lost somewhere between zero and infinity.

—KATON

SUBJECT'S PREFACE

.

From the beginning the truth was present, expressing itself in myriad forms. Had I the courage I would have perceived it from the start, saving myself from the endless repetition of life, the suffering and confusion, but most of all from the uncertainty which will plague mankind throughout eternity. But no man wishes to know himself, not even those who preach such a doctrine, for within each person is an aversion for the truth, a hatred for what we really are. And so we must play our games, hiding from the destiny we must one day face.

No one knows the cause of the incident—the action which triggered the final crisis. Explanations and stories differ, yet the outcome was the same. Somehow it had occurred and we were powerless to resist. It was for this reason that we joined together to undermine the Structure. And it was because of our convergence that the story turned tragic.

My central presence suggests in no way my importance or involvement, for I myself, played only a minor role in the affair. However I recall it as I saw it. And I must stress the point that, though I am the subject of the account, I am not its author. The writer abides in anonymity. No one knows who or what is responsible for the story. Having taken no part in its transcription I simply endorse its veracity.

Who can say when it began? Things of this sort are never clearly derived. Gradually they take shape, growing until finally recognized. When I first noticed its presence it was already glaringly obvious, invading every action and every thought. But looking back further in time to the first vague feelings of distress, it seems to have happened then, when as a small child I witnessed the arrival of a strange guest. It was then that it had all begun.

Chapter One:
THE MESSENGER

_____

He woke me to a waking dream.

—SUBJECT

FORTHRIGHT, with unity of soul and purpose, he trudged up the snow and ice-covered slope. And though each step brought him closer to death, it also brought him one step closer to his destination. I watched from the balcony porch, gazing down upon his slow, yet steady progress: a uniformed blackness moving across a field of white, one spot marring the frozen serenity. It was a brilliance in which he himself was the sole contrast.

He traveled in a daze, not once looking at the crystalline powder through which he made his way, for one purpose compelled him to the end, yet I was uncertain what that end might be. My doubts vanished as he opened the garden gate and banged repeatedly upon our front door. The household had been roused.

I scampered down the stairs and excitedly opened the massive, wooden door. A sudden coldness invaded the room, penetrating the warmth and comfort of our home. The icy air sent a chill down my back as I stood exposed to the presence of our unknown guest. He was inured to life. His obsession was his goal. And now that it was over he was ready to collapse. He stood bracing himself against the doorway, each moment draining him of life and energy. Nevertheless, with stoic fortitude and dignity, he informed us of the message he carried for me.

"But there must be some mistake," said my mother, wrapping me protectively in her arms. "The only person here by that name is our child."

He gazed down at me as I gazed up at him. I was amazed to find him snow-blind from his quest. His eyes suddenly lost their strength, releasing their hold as they stared vacantly through and beyond. Overwhelmed by the darkness he abandoned all hope, sinking to his knees and collapsing on the floor. His last words were mine, his last message: the time has come.

Ever since then my life has never been the same, for his death seemed to have opened a door to another world, another dimension which existed side by side with the mundane. Deep inside lurked the suspicion that life was not as simple as it seemed, that things were not really as they appeared. This feeling haunted me through childhood so that I could no longer run and play with other children, for the memory kept recurring—the tortured face, the pain and suffering of his journey.

The experience dampened my life, forcing me to withdraw from the carefree, innocent world of my youth. I hid in the dark recesses of a nightmare world, nightmares which grew in intensity, nightmares without end that began controlling my life. They did not fade as I grew older (as was the case with other children), but on the contrary became so insidious, so terrifying that each day I dreaded the approaching darkness of night, for all my dreams were filled with horror. But strangely enough I became used to this insanity, accepting it as a normal course of life. I built up a resistance to what I believed had to be. It came as a surprise when I discovered that others slept without nightmares, that most people had only an occasional bad dream.

My friends grew concerned when I told them of what I lived through each night, of the strange absence of any pleasant dreams, of any dreams which were even slightly tolerable. But that is not to say the situations never occurred. Many times I would dream of happiness and pleasure, but this served only to intensify the violence which followed. They were a mockery and a deception, and each time they occurred the air grew ominous for what was to come. I began wondering what was wrong with me, why I should live so differently from others. I withdrew even further, guarding myself against the demon I was sure was in control.

I became a zombie-insomniac: dead to the world—unable or unwilling to sleep. For sleep was the only state in which I was vulnerable to attack. Sleep was the realm over which my nemesis reigned. The sleepless nights disoriented my life, for with each new day began a struggle to remain awake. Each day was a misery and exhaustion. My demon's onslaughts redoubled. He knew that I was weakening, that soon I could no longer resist. On the day of my Structural evaluation came his final attempt. After being informed of my loss in standings I returned home and fell struggling into a deep, unwanted sleep.

His familiars wasted no time in ferreting me out, yet this time, too tired to run, I simply hid as best I could. They came in strong and cunning animal forms. From my lofty tree-perch I looked down upon the hunting grounds. I climbed stealthily for a more concealed position. If I couldn't see them maybe they couldn't see me. A piercing pain suddenly shot through my arm! I recoiled and was greeted by the sharp fangs of a tree snake with raised head, on-guard, ready for another strike. The poison invaded my being. Within moments the world began reeling. I lost my balance and plummeted from the tree. My body twisted and spun as I plunged to the earth. On impact the bed jolted me awake! I rose tremulously, but as I tried to stand and turn on the lights, the dizziness and weakness allowed the floor to give way. I collapsed again, this time into unconsciousness and a new dream. Would it never end?

* * * * *

The voice had been whispering for quite some time, but only now was I aware of the words.

"Wake up," she said softly. I struggled weakly to open my eyes. The blurred vision became vaguely discernible, but the light was too strong, forcing me to strain to see her presence. A young nurse dressed in a rainbow-colored uniform was hovering by the bed, calmly observing my struggle to consciousness. On seeing me awaken she smiled with relief.

"I see you've decided to wake up," she said cheerfully. But her words had no effect. I remained motionless and silent, drained of life. I was light-headed and dizzy. My body was clammy and flushed by chills.

"Now that you're awake," she continued, "who should we notify?"

I reflected for a moment, but the sickness must have affected my mind, for my memory was distorted and incomplete. With embarrassment I weakly shrugged my shoulders.

"Any relatives or friends?" she asked in surprise.

Pondering for a few moments, I remembered someone I had really cared for. At any other time the mere thought of her gave me a feeling of loving warmth and comfort, yet now there was nothing. She could die for all I cared. But how could this be? I tried desperately to rekindle the feelings, to bring back some assurance of reality, but they were gone. What I thought would never die was dead, and I felt myself being pulled into another world.

"No one?" she queried in sad astonishment. But I was slipping away too quickly, and in a moment I was gone.

The visions of my delirium seemed absurd, and yet no more absurd than the delirium of my life, for somehow, refusing to be dismissed, was the uneasy feeling that the madness was meaningful. One recurring dream placed me in a theater of darkness. Upon the isolated stage were a small table and a light where an old man sat reading a book. Many times I dreamt the same dream before discovering the title, *The Time Has Come*, by Katon. As always I asked whether I could read the book. But the old man indicated he was not yet finished, implying I could have it when he was done. I stood patiently awaiting his conclusion. The time passed slowly. The minutes struggled to become hours. I stood catatonic, a cold sweat covering my face. I felt sick to my stomach, and yet I lingered on. Occasionally out of impatience I asked if he was through, but he never was. I was ready to collapse and yet I remained, for there was nowhere else to go, nothing else to do, for all was void. Suddenly, unable to stand, I dropped to the floor hoping the ordeal was over, yet the old man was still reading unperturbed in his chair. For hours I lay watching as he turned a page every few minutes, each turn a tormenting click within the empty clockwork of my mind. Finally out of chance or out of mercy a soft voice would break through.

"You'll be all right," she would whisper. "It's all over." And I would awaken. Each time was worse than the last, and each time I grew more indebted for her services. This time, however, the weakness was gone, for I realized that my body was now paralyzed. Though unable to move at least the indifference had vanished, making me more inquisitive than usual, though no less immobile.

"Who sent you?" I asked. "The Structure?"

"Impossible," she laughed, "a private concern, Dreams, Incorporated." I had never heard of such an organization.

"Who are you?" I asked in befuddlement. I could feel myself losing consciousness, for my lucid moments lasted only seconds.

"Iris," she replied with a smile, "a caretaker of Dreams, Incorporated."

"Who's Iris?" I mumbled while being pulled into a delirium. I now had no idea what I meant, but she replied anyway.

"I am," said a voice out of the void. "That is who I am."

* * * * *

The madness returned. The senseless, yet frightening scenes passed before my eyes: a Stickman pulling and tearing at his hair, a Duckling being beaten and half-drowned. The absurd was my playground, but I wasn't having any fun. I was the center of existence surrounded by insanity.

As always I returned to the dark stage and stood waiting patiently, yearning for the moment my predecessor would finish. Page after page, hour after hour I waited with nothing else to do, sickened by the emptiness of the encompassing void.

Suddenly the old man closed the book. I was overjoyed as he rose from his seat, offering me his place and his book. It had finally happened: the time had come. I settled down with anticipation and opened to the first page. It was blank! I turned to the next page. It too was blank. I flipped through the entire book, but it was nothing but blank pages! I screamed in frustration when the old man grabbed the book and, laughing like a madman, threw it off into the darkness. I awoke with his laughter echoing through my mind, a demonic laughter I would never forget.

* * * * *

The paralysis had vanished. I could move freely, more freely than ever before. I jumped out of bed with unusual vigor. The dizziness and chills were also gone. Not only had I recovered, but I had gained a new feeling of awareness and power. I had come into being. The time had truly come.

But where was Iris? The nurse who had restored me to life had vanished just like a rainbow. The modesty of the generous. Seeing me recover, she must have left to avoid any show of gratitude, for she knew that I now owed her my life. However this was not the end of it, for not only must I thank her, but I was also curious about the nature of my illness. I dressed and started off for the Structural Hall of Records. There I could pinpoint the location and origin of Iris.

What made me so sick, I wondered to myself on the way? Was it a developing sickness that caused the dream? Or, as uncanny as it may be, did the dream cause the sickness? The snakebite of my dream coincided so exactly with my illness that, though reason objected, it could not be ignored. And what about Katon? As fantastic as it seemed, could there be such an author, a book and an author revealed to me in a dream? Answering these questions was my only concern, for after my ordeal nothing else seemed to matter.

I entered the Structural Hall of Records and proceeded to the rows of files listing alphabetically all existing organizations from the tiniest shop to the largest corporation. I looked under "D," but nothing was there. According to the records there was no such company as "Dreams, Incorporated." I was dismayed by this bureaucratic oversight and subsequently shifted my attention to the files of Structural Subjects.

Cross-referenced under "Mathematical Symbols" I located the key to determining Iris's point of origin. However to my chagrin I discovered not the tangible identity paper containing practical information on a Subject's location and destiny, but rather a vague essay by some obscure professor contending that a geometric ray is composed of an infinite quantity of points which cannot be pinned down, arrested, or made tangible in any way.

The treatise furthermore educed that these points are mere theoretical existents which together form a concrete expression and direction and in some cases even vectors, but nevertheless existents which by themselves are simply vaguely defined constructs without physical dimensions or substance. Such theoretical forces are never clearly derived, but simply assimilate into an infinite whole at which point they are finally recognized. Furthermore, a geometric ray can be broken down into partial line segments, and these segments can be further subdivided into even smaller units. And yet each unit, no matter how large or small, contains an infinite quantity of points within itself. Thus the ray is not only an infinitely expansive whole, but also an infinitely subdivisible entity composed of an infinite quantity of infinities. What's more, the ray as an arrow directs a theoretical extension which must, by mathematical definition, necessarily occur. Hence the geometric existence of the ray beyond its physical limitations is an axiom maintained by the ray's own existence!

In such a manner the ray is tantamount to a

physical correlate of infinity. For an eternal recurrence and assimilation, no matter how infinitely small, will by definition result in infinite extension. Consequently an infinite distance (normally impossible to traverse) will necessarily be traversed provided the direction is correct. However, the slightest, most minute, infinitely negligible deflection will, through the nature of infinity, result in gross inaccuracies. With an infinitely extending ray traversing an infinite theoretical distance the smallest miscalculation anywhere along the path will eventually result in enormous discrepancies. The ray must therefore be infinitely exact and always on target, otherwise it will never reach its appointed goal, and an infinite extension will thus become an infinite digression.

I was baffled. I could neither interpret nor intuit the significance of this misplaced thesis. Therefore I returned the Subject's paper to its original position and closed the file. I left the Structural Hall of Records more confused than when I had started. My sole remaining lead was to search the Library. Perhaps there I would discover The Time Has Come. For even if Iris and her organization had eluded me at least Katon and his book might exist. But my failure with "Dreams, Incorporated" made me doubt my own dream. I was at a loss to explain the discrepancy, for I was certain that was the name she had spoken. Who was she, I wondered. Where did she come from? And how could she have stayed with me while I was indifferent to her presence, and as soon as I needed her, abandon me without word?

It was bound to happen sooner or later. Only chance held me from my discovery. As I passed a chronometer I noticed the date. I froze in my tracks. Only one day had passed since the night of my sickness! My Structural evaluation was yesterday! Yet weeks had seemed to pass within my delirium. How many times had I awakened, seemingly to a new day? How many days had seemingly come and gone?

I stopped a passer-by and asked his interpretation of the time. With subtle gestures and strange attitudes he indicated that the time was indeed correct. Yet I refused to believe it was all a dream—the sickness, the delirium, the paralysis, the awakenings. And what about Iris? She was too real, too authentic to be merely an image from my mind, yet how else could it be explained? For the distorted passage of time, the convincing reality of my sickness could only be the result of some elaborate nightmare. Or could it be something more? Only one hope remained. If there were such an author as Katon, an author revealed to me in a dream, then everything would be redeemed. But what would it prove?—that somewhere my subconscious had heard and retained a strange name, that in the midst of madness it was incorporated into a dream? Yet, despite my skepticism, if Katon did exist all was not lost, for deep inside I felt that somehow all could be explained.

I meandered in circles for some time without reaching the Library. And suddenly it dawned on me that I was lost. Strange as it seems now, without any idea of the Library's location I simply started off with perfect confidence in reaching my destination. Having never been there before, nor having the vaguest hint or feeling of its direction, I was at a loss to explain my impulsive movements. Yet strangely enough I had set out for the Structural Hall of Records in the same manner and had found it with ease. Just as naturally had I set out for the Library, but now, as logic would predict, found myself lost. Yet why was I so surprised? How could I leave without directions and expect to find my way by chance? I stopped and asked a passer-by for directions.

"To what?" she puzzled in disbelief.

"The Library," I repeated.

"Never heard of it," she shrugged and quickly walked off.

"The Library?" said another passer-by in bewilderment. "There's a dime store with books at the end of the passage." I thanked him and proceeded to the store, knowing full well that it was useless, yet having nowhere else to go. I entered the shop and immediately noticed a stand of popular fiction near the entrance.

"The Library?" said the clerk as I asked him for directions.

"A literary complex in which reading and research takes place." He seemed puzzled and so I elaborated. "It's a large structure filled with myriad passages and stories. People can read them there as they are or take them beyond the premises."

"The only place remotely similar is the Structural Bookstore. But borrow them!" he laughed. "You have to pay for them through the nose, and you can't read them there. There is no loitering." He provided directions and I started to leave when he motioned to his shelves. "I have some books here," he said sheepishly in hopes of selling some cheap work of fiction. I smiled discreetly and hurried my departure.

I proceeded to the Structural Bookstore, doubting that I would find the book of my dreams. Yet I hoped that someone may have at least heard of its author. After only a brief interval I arrived at the store.

"Can I help you?" asked the salesgirl seated at the front counter. She almost appeared to be real. Yet her mesmerizing beauty made me realize that she was only a dream—a past dream that I had dreamt while only a child. I responded nevertheless.

"Yes," I replied eagerly, "I'm looking for *The Time Has Come*, by Katon." As expected she seemed puzzled and distraught.

"How do you spell that name?" she enquired while thumbing through her reference, her casual movements in time to the erotic swinging of her leg.

"There's no such author," she concluded curtly, closing the file and uncrossing her legs, then re-crossing them with the opposing leg swinging slowly, the extended toes moving sensually up and down.

"But I'm not positive of the spelling," I objected. "I only heard it spoken."

"There's no name even faintly similar," she remarked dismissively. "Nor is there any such book by that title."

"Are you certain?" I pleaded, unable to accept the consequences of her judgment.

"Of course!" she replied indignantly. A few customers glanced up from the stories they were browsing. "We have every book that has ever been written. If you can't find it here then it doesn't exist."

The manager arrived to settle the dispute.

"What's the problem?" he asked the salesgirl, slipping his hand over her knee.

"This person is looking for The Time Has Come. He refuses to believe that it doesn't exist."

The manager took me aside as though in confidence. "The book," he explained, "is simply a figment of your imagination. Why don't you look around? I'm sure you'll find something else you'd like."

I wandered through the premises, scanning the long racks of books, but there was nothing but popular fiction, nothing but cheap, dime-store trash. As I glanced through the inventory I noticed that, though the plots might vary in time and place, their endings, though with different characters, were essentially the same. And if this were not enough, the repetition was further magnified.

"What's this?" I demanded of the salesgirl. "Why are there so many copies of the same story?" For entire cases of a single book lay waiting to be unpacked. Her forehead wrinkled. Her eyelashes fluttered in disdain.

"Lots of people want the same story," she answered suspiciously. "What's so unusual about that?"

I shook my head in dismay and returned to inventory the books. *The Time Won't Come. The Time Will Come. The Time To Come. The Time Never Comes.* And an empty space upon the shelf. A card in the back said: "Time to Reorder. OUT OF STOCK." And in hand-written letters: *The Time Has Come*, along with the contact's address. I grabbed the evidence and demanded an explanation.

"What's this?" I challenged with smug contempt.

The manager, who was preoccupied squeezing the salesgirl's thigh, began trembling as he confronted the truth.

"We've been infiltrated!" he exclaimed. "It's the Revolutionists—they're at it again. It's a joke on their part. It's a play to undermine the Structure. But take my word for it—there is no such book— no such book . . ." he rattled on as he continued to squeeze.

Joke or no joke, the thought that others knew of Katon was reassuring, for he was more than just a figment of my mind. I left for the address and noticed that it was in an unfamiliar area of the Structure, though all areas of the Structure now seemed unfamiliar. While walking I reflected over the strangeness of what was happening. Somehow everything of my past had lost its meaning. My friends and acquaintances seemed strangers to me. Worst of all was the absence of any affinity to my former world. Everything there seemed remote and unreal as though all part of some past dream. I seemed to have finally awakened from a long, slumbering sleep, from an illness that left the world cold and unsure. I realized that I would never again feel at home, that I was condemned forever to spiritual exile, and yet the feeling and hope remained that somewhere, at some indefinite future time I would find a position in life I could call my own.

Eventually I found myself within a group of Subjects clustering about someone of importance and prestige. He seemed irritated and fled inside the auditorium before which we were gathered. The excitement died as the group disbanded. Moving closer to the entrance I noticed a poster with the words:

TONIGHT AT 12 A.M.
FOR INSOMNIACS AND NIGHT OWLS
THE PROFESSOR'S THEORY OF ACCELERATION
BRING YOUR OWN REFRESHMENTS
ENTER THROUGH SUB-CELLAR Z

Where had I heard it before? The Professor and his theory seemed vaguely familiar, but I could recall nothing of the circumstances which linked us together. Perhaps it was a premonition of a predestined future. Or perhaps it was a forgotten source of contact. Whatever the case, whether from the past or from the future, somehow I knew that our lives were closely bound. For feelings of excitement and intrigue, of camaraderie in the face of unknown dangers stirred deep within my soul. His theory aroused memories of mystery and adventure in imaginary worlds beyond conscious extension.

I resolved to return and attend the lecture, noting the time and location in my dubious memory. I then continued my journey and found Katon's contact address. I climbed the wooden staircase to find the door wide open. My contact was oblivious to my presence. He remained seated at a table totally absorbed within his book. Suddenly, he glanced up and recoiled in fright. Whatever demon he saw was beyond imagining. The terror in his eyes drove me back in fear. But eventually, perceiving the mistaken identity, he calmed as his questioning eyes tried to discern my appearance.

"What do you want?" he asked in an attempt toward composure.

"The Time Has Come," I responded in order to trigger another reaction. His eyes lit up as though we were lifelong friends.

"Come on in," he said eagerly. "Tell me what you know, and don't leave out anything." We relaxed as I related the events of the day—the dream, the fruitless search for the book, and finally my discovery of his card at the bookstore. He listened with nostalgia.

"You're lucky to have such dreams," he remarked. "Not many people do. Hardly anyone believes the legend of Katon. Most have never heard of him."

"But what about you?" I asked with curiosity. "How did you first come to know of him?"

"In a more conventional sense. It was part of my job as assistant to the Professor. Katon's peregrinations helped map out the area beyond the West Walls. It inspired the Professor's Theory of Acceleration."

The remainder of the day was spent in conversation. For hours he related what he knew of Katon and the Professor. Frequently he referred to strange books and documents which, in all my wildest fancies, I never imagined could exist. According to them, Katon was a legendary explorer, discoverer of a hidden dimension of existence. Through extended surveys he surmounted the plane of normal life, revealing his visions to a world slumbering within the facade of the Structure. Most took him to be a crackpot. But to some he had stirred a fire that had been smoldering since the manifestation of the Structure. Unable to compromise, disdaining the

Structural benefits and petty comforts, this rebellious group found hope with Katon. He became their visionary leader and prophet. His philosophy caused wide-spread dissension and eventually armed revolt. But this revolutionary circle was no match for the magnitude of the Structure. Constant fighting was all that was assured with no decisive victory for either faction in sight, for the Structure had inexhaustible resources. Anything destroyed was immediately repaired or replaced. On the other hand the Revolutionists has the stratagem of secrecy and espionage—the advantages of agility and mobility, to strike and run, to insidiously merge with and destroy the enemy without warning. Even seemingly total defeat of the Revolutionists was followed by an eventual re-grouping and relocation. Both sides were apparently invincible, and so the fighting continued. As a result, Katon was labeled a traitor by the Structure. He became a fugitive and, along with his followers, was forced underground perhaps even to the level of the Sub-Basement. Eventually everyone, including his followers, lost touch with him. He had vanished without trace.

"Remember," he cautioned, "these are only myths and legends. There are a variety of other stories and interpretations." He then related a multitude of varying and contradictory accounts which resulted in total confusion. "Personally," he explained, "I believe Katon is now beyond the West Walls."

"But that's impossible," I argued. "No one can live for long out there. It's alien and inhospitable. It's a virtual wasteland."

"Do you believe that" he chuckled. "Or is that

what others have brainwashed you into believing?"

"What's the Professor's involvement?" I asked, dismissing the poignancy of his question and changing the subject. He smiled in triumph.

"That's just it!" he exclaimed. "What links Katon and the Professor is their exploration into other dimensions. They're one of the few who ever purposely ventured beyond the West Walls. And also the only ones who returned with any semblance of sanity." I nodded, for I knew it was no coincidence which had brought us together. It was a cosmic plan being mapped by something greater.

"But what makes the Professor immune?" I queried. "Why isn't the Structure after him? Why wasn't he labeled a traitor?"

"For the simple reason that most fail to comprehend his position. What he says is clear. I understand it, but few others do. As a result his books find no market. As it is with Katon's works, most bookstores don't even carry them. And yet," he added with an enigmatic smile, "there are some underground bookstores and libraries which do."

And so our conversation went on through the night. We got on so well, our discussion so exciting that we instantly realized the bonds of our friendship. The time passed quickly. It was getting late! I noticed that the lecture on Acceleration would soon begin and rose to leave.

"But aren't you coming?" I asked on seeing that he remained seated. "Doesn't the Professor need you?"

"I've heard it a hundred times," he quipped, shaking his head. "And the Professor only needs himself.

Better hurry or they'll start without you. And come back any time!" he called out as I left.

I began retracing my steps to the auditorium, backtracking along the path which I had traveled earlier in the day. And yet, even with a set course, I failed to reach my destination. I was certain my movements were correct. This was indeed the route by which I had stumbled upon the Professor. Nevertheless I was progressing nowhere. All my efforts were in vain. I realized that I would be late and quickened my pace, but this led only to accelerated meandering and increasing confusion. I was a fool! I was a malingerer! Had I only known the journey was so extensive I would have started off sooner. But now, because of my ignorance, I was destined to be late.

"Slow down," said a stranger. "Why such a rush?" I shrugged my shoulders, not wishing to be detained by conversation. "It's too bad what happened," he said with sympathy. I stopped to face him.

"What's too bad?" I asked.

"Your Structural evaluation!" he said in disbelief. "Your loss of standings. Your recent illness." Only now did I recognize him as one of my colleagues. "You'd better watch it," he warned. "If I were you I'd either get back to work or back to sleep. You know we have classes tomorrow."

But his words meant nothing, for all that mattered was my goal. I extricated myself and descended the first stairway to the Sub-Basement. It was another world down there buried below the edifice of the Structure. All the detritus and cast-offs lay molding and decaying away—prime breeding ground for spawning diseased monsters.

I began forging my way through the mess, but progress was slow and difficult, for junk was heaped about in tumbled stacks and piles—banished to a forgotten realm. Old relics and rubbish which had outlasted their usefulness were stored, or more likely discarded and scattered amidst the dust and cobwebs.

Unwillingly I began recalling the ghost stories and superstitions of childhood—all of which were centered here in the remotest, most desolate area of the Structure. Laughable as it may seem at another time, all alone without protection I gradually began to walk faster. Absurdly enough I felt that someone or something was following. Not just ghosts or demons. Why, I never believed in such childish superstition, but there could be outcasts and murderers, madmen and Revolutionists.

On hearing something move I broke into a run. Now I was sure something was following! Glancing back I could see some hazy form thrashing its way through the half-darkness, sending unseen objects crashing to the floor. I fled for my life on the verge of a breakdown. My only hope was to find an exit. It seemed forever before I spotted a doorway up ahead. On rushing through I noticed, above the entrance, the words: Sub-Cellar Z. I slammed the wooden door, turned the flimsy lock, and looked for the exit. But there wasn't one! I was panicking into madness when suddenly the nightmare demon began smashing the rotten door. Pressing against it for reinforcement, I scanned about for something, anything, any way of escape. Yet the only thing in the tiny storage room was a closet door. There was no way out, but at least to delay the end, I dashed for the closet. Yet to my surprise and relief the door opened upon a stairway! Suddenly the demon burst into the room, lunging from behind as I scrambled up the stairs, grasping at my feet as I leapt from stair to stair. It was almost upon me when I stumbled upon an exit and, with a final burst of energy, rushed through and slammed the door.

Chapter Two:
BEYOND THE WEST WALLS

Truth seeker, challenging truth only when truth challenges you— subtlest self-deception.

—KATON

THE LECTURE WAS IN PROGRESS. The Theory of Acceleration had already begun. Yet I was surprised to find no more than a dozen people scattered about the huge auditorium. I felt an emptiness and isolation as I surveyed the sorrowful handful of students. Where were the crowds? Where were the admirers that had greeted the Professor with such enthusiasm? Of course it was late, but what better time to initiate such a radical movement? Such nocturnal transitions should never be clearly derived, but must be affected gradually, growing until finally recognized. And yet how could it be recognized with no one around? Dismayed by the lack of presence, but not wishing to disturb the proceedings, I settled quietly in a back seat and attended the Professor:

"Take the case of transferring an object from point A to point Z. First we must establish whether such an object does indeed exist, for it would be absurd to move an imaginary object from place to place. Granted that the existence of the object was an axiom to begin with, and that without such an object there would be no problem in the first place, one is still tempted to wonder whether there is such an object and whether such a problem does, in fact, exist. It is known that mere appearance does not guarantee actual existence (for example dreams and hallucinations). Therefore it is possible that after great amounts of time and energy are expended in moving the object from A to Z, one may suddenly discover that such an object does not even exist! One might then naturally assume that despair and a sense of futility would be the result, but it must be remembered that without the object, the situation and the problem would vanish without trace. Therefore, lacking contrary information, one must yield to the Theory of Parsimony and accept the existence of the object on the basis of its appearance. However, one must also stipulate that this first qualification and risk of logic was necessary in order to resolve the dilemma and begin the first stage of the experiment.

"Taking for granted the existence of the object and confronted with the task of moving it from A to Z, one now comes to the logically inevitable question: is there such a thing as motion? Or, in other words, does the possibility of displacement exist? Or, to make it even simpler, is the object permanently affixed to point A or is it capable of being elsewhere? One must also ask the concomitant question: does point Z exist? The answers to these questions are essential in resolving the problem, for why attempt to move to point Z if no such point even exists, and why attempt to move at all if there is no such thing as motion? But a negative response to either of these questions brings about the same positive results. For if Z does not exist, then the distance between A and Z also does not exist. In a flash the distance vanishes and, in a sense, Z has become A and the object has reached its destination without moving. The problem has been solved, though the very existence of point Z destroys its own solution. On the second point, if the process of motion does not exist, then again the experiment is over without having begun. For if there is no such thing as motion, then the possibility of moving to Z was an illusion and the problem as such had never existed. Seeing the problem solve itself with negative answers to the previous questions, one must now look to the alternative positions.

"Taking for granted the existence of the object, the points, and the process of motion, one must now begin the second stage of the experiment. Seeing the problem to be the movement of the object from A to Z, the next logical question arises—why? Why move the object from point A to Z? The answer is simple—because. For the feeling of discontent itself caused the formulation of the problem. If one has no desire to move the object to Z, then no such problem exists. We can wash our hands of the whole rotten mess!"

I was startled from a light sleep by a sudden harshness in the Professor's voice. However, my surprise gave way to my fatigue as I quickly fell back half asleep, but my eyes were open just enough to take vague notice of the Professor's growing agitation:

"Taking for granted a desire to move the object to point Z, one must now plan the best path to travel. This of course means taking into consideration the time involved, the distance traveled, the most efficient course, and also the method of Acceleration. If one fails to consider these aspects carefully, then even with the greatest amount of time and energy one may still fail in moving the object to its appointed goal. Knowing all this, how then can any sane person start from point A and find himself at point B? Why is it that invariably one does not reach the destination for which one aims, but instead, travels to countless other points in countless other planes and dimension, traversing haphazardly, backtracking, meandering, nearing point Z then suddenly veering off toward some other fanciful goal? I believe the reason for this randomness is simple. No one really wishes to move the object to point Z, but wishes merely to move. And if by chance, after consuming much time and energy, the object returns again to point A, it is of no matter, for motion is the only thing for which the object cares. It is an insatiable process without beginning or end. Now that I see you have all fallen asleep I may as well conclude."

These last words were spoken with such contempt and mockery that we were all startled from our sleep and were wide awake as the Professor ended the proceedings:

"As any wise man knows, the shortest distance between any two points is a straight line."

With the conclusion of his speech the Professor stomped off the stage. The students excitedly discussed the theory, pretending they had heard the entire lecture. Nervous and embarrassed, the announcer stepped onto the platform and addressed the audience:

"We have been honored by the Professor's appearance here tonight. I hope you've enjoyed the discourse on his revolutionary Theory of Acceleration. The Professor has explained that this was the most simplistic view of his theory. His intentions were to proceed to the more advanced and intricate aspects, however he now believes Acceleration to be beyond conveyance. Therefore he regrets to announce that he will no longer appear in public."

Disappointment flashed over everyone's face, but deep inside I knew his position was correct. I need simply seek out the strange libraries that carried his books. The announcer continued:

"One movement from now our guest speaker will be Iris, a representative of Dreams, Incorporated. Thank you for coming. Due to the late hour all Structural exits have been secured. Excuse the inconvenience, but please leave through the open windows."

How comical to see such serious students clambering to squeeze through the narrow windows, but I had no time for levity, for the memory of the lecture was quickly fading. And I must remember now, before leaving my seat, before distracted from thought. Otherwise, like a dream it would soon vanish. It was imperative. It was vital to remember the lecture, yet all I could recall were the Professor's last words. "As any wise man knows, the shortest distance between any two points is a straight line." What was it he was saying? Deep inside I knew. It was there, yet I failed to make it appear.

Unreflectively I observed the student's droll movements as I struggled to remember. "A," I thought to myself. It had something to do with the letter "A." "A," I repeated to myself. "A, B." I felt it vaguely and so I began. "A, B, C, D"—No. That was wrong. It's too long. "Alphabetically arranged," I said for no reason. "Alphabet," I said slowly and thoughtfully as though deciphering some secret code. "Alpha—" I began to repeat, stopping halfway through the word. "Alpha-bet," I said, breaking it into two syllables. I felt it coming again. "Alpha, beta," I said suddenly with encouragement, "gamma." What came after "gamma?" I struggled to recall my math and science. Then suddenly I knew! "Delta, epsilon." But what came next? I couldn't recall. Had I ever learned the sixth letter? Was it ever part of the Structural curriculum? I could only remember the first five, for I never seemed to use other symbols in problem-solving. My predicament came to an abrupt end by noticing that the last of the students had squeezed through the windows. I was forced to leave my seat and problem behind—or so I thought. After all, I couldn't remain alone in a deserted auditorium—could I?

I proceeded to the windows and climbed through to the other side, but there was no one there. No one cared to linger in the arctic chill. In the wild, it was every man for himself. I had been abandoned in the cold darkness and soon hurried off along the snowy path. But which way had they gone? There was no telling, for the tracks went everywhere. It was up to me to decide my own path.

As I advanced through the night my world soon became a maze. The path merged with others and then broke off in different directions. Constantly they attempted to carry me away in misdirection, but I refused to allow myself to be lured from the Structure. I kept close to the building, found the first entrance, and tried the door. It was locked! It couldn't be! It was a mistake! I pounded upon the door though I knew no one would hear. The pounding reverberated through my soul, for there was only one place in the Structure where passages were secured. I gazed down the unbroken facade of buildings and saw there were no windows. The West Walls! Somehow I was on the forbidden side of the Structure! Strange stories filled me with horror and anxiety. Images of insanity flashed through my mind: stickmen in revolt; demons of all shapes and sizes; ducklings running away from home. This was the rumored land of madness. It was here that all mind-altering experiments were conducted. It was here that legendary revolutions were plotted and hatched.

I hurried back along the path to the auditorium, for at least there I would be immune to the mysterious effect of this land. My problem was three-fold: to avoid dying of exposure; to find my way back into the Structure; and to escape being affected by this unpredictable environment. For even those briefly exposed beyond the West Walls were treated as misfits and outcasts.

As I had traveled longer than necessary to reach the lecture hall, I stopped and scanned the solid Structure from which I had emerged. Either the auditorium was gone or I had assumed the wrong direction among the maze of paths. I had no idea which was the case, nor did it matter, for I would soon succumb to the cold and my problems would end. As I stood and contemplated my fate, the stillness, the haunting emptiness of this world struck me and drained me of life. Nothing moved. Nothing made a sound. Even the gusty wind had died. Yet in this desolate landscape came the sound of footsteps crunching through the snow. Alarmed, but too far gone to be afraid, I crouched behind a large, dead bush, for caution was necessary in a land where Revolutionists and madmen lurked within every shadow. And at night everywhere was a shadow.

Reassured by the footsteps which would soon end my predicament, I patiently awaited the strange, night-wanderer. I listened calmly to the steps which crushed the ice and snow against the hard, rock path. The footsteps rang out through the icy air, breaking the oppressive silence of the night. I peered through the leafless branches and saw the black boots and trousers of a uniformed man come to a halt before the bush. Hesitant and unsure, the shiny black boots crunched a few steps into the layer of snow, stopped, then turned and waited. A strong, yet light-hearted voice broke the momentary silence. It was a human voice in an alien world, a voice filled with friendliness and humor.

"If you hide long enough, dying from exposure is painless."

I stepped out from my lair, but then lost all courage, for the man's uniform and bearing distinguished him as a high-ranking official.

"The Professor's lecture," I stammered. "They made us leave through the windows, but the Structure was locked."

"Calm yourself," he suggested on seeing my reaction. "I'm only the night watchman." With relief I tried to ease the pounding in my heart, and after a moment I recovered from my shock. "What makes you want to return?" he asked with curiosity.

"What a naive question," I thought to myself. It was an absurd question, an impossible question, for where else was I to go? I shrugged in response and he nodded in sad understanding. Resigned to the task, he started back along the path, motioning me to follow. As I watched him march through the snow in his long, heavy overcoat and sturdy, winter boots, I suddenly felt the cold I had forgotten. The pain pierced my fingers and toes. My face and ears felt like they were cracking and burning. I caught up and walked along his side. With hands in pockets I succumbed to uncontrollable fits of shivering.

"Only a little farther," he reassured on noticing my discomfort, then he laughed and shook his head. "The Professor and his lectures. How he appoints the time." He pulled a notebook from his pocket and scribbled some words. "See her," he said, tearing off a slip of paper. "Take some of her courses and forget about the Professor. You'll meet him soon enough." I stuffed the note into my pocket as I stumbled along.

"Here we are," he remarked dismally as we came to a ventilation shaft on the Structural facade. "If you're sure this is where you want to go." He slid the screen aside and beckoned me to enter. "Just crawl to the end and push open the vent on the other side."

I followed his instructions and climbed headlong into the confining darkness. He watched as I journeyed partway through the system. "Don't forget to see her," he called out with a voice made hollow by the effect of the crawlway. "Tell Iris that Katon sent you," his words echoed. Katon! The name flashed through my mind arousing memories of dream worlds and secret doctrines, prophecies and future goals. I turned just in time to see the screen slide back over the opening, shutting me off from the alien world of the West Walls. Regrettably I moved on to the end of the passage, feeling my way through the total darkness.

So this was Katon, legendary explorer and Structural Revolutionist. And he was alive! After his disappearance many presumed him dead. Most, who had never seen him, claimed that he had never existed. Unable to find any of his writings as proof, the skeptics believed that Katon was a myth. And though everyone was aware of him, only a small circle of followers believed he was real. And out of that circle only a few believed he was still alive, for the rumor spread that he had been murdered by the Structure. Others claimed he was incognito. Still others were convinced that he had passed beyond the West Walls. I now knew it to be true.

As to the disappearance of his writings, those who believed in him claimed that they had been not only banned, but burned by the Structure. But rumors held that fragments and forbidden copies still exist in secret libraries. Whatever the case, Katon was alive! And I would tell everyone of this night and of the honor of his presence, for even before his disappearance he was seldom seen, and only by rare and fortunate individuals.

I journeyed through the darkness of the crawlway until I saw a faint light in the distance. Was it imagination? Was it illusion? Painfully I crawled forward on hands and knees, bruised and sore from my strenuous movements. My nocturnal vision was apparently correct, for the brightness grew proportionally to the distance traveled.

Reaching the light, I looked down from a screened vent onto an immense stage surrounded by darkness with a small table and light in the center. Upon the table was an unfinished manuscript whose unbound pages lay scattered in disarray. A sudden impulse made me pass through the vent, climb down to the stage and investigate the nature of this incomplete work. It seemed to be a textbook on mathematical expressions by some obscure professor. The pages were disordered. Some were perhaps missing. Thus the structure was violated. The meaning was out of context. However I did manage to capture the gist of the story. The story?

It was a geometric story about a mathematical progression into infinity. The plot was centered about an algebraic proof. The subject, a mathematical symbol. The given, a variable with a value unknown. The form, by necessity, was the first person narrative. Thus it was as confusing as any subjective account. Nevertheless, picking a page at random, I proceeded to read it as it was.

I journeyed through the darkness of the crawl-way until I saw a faint light in the distance. Was it imagination? Was it illusion? Painfully I crawled forward on hands and knees, bruised and sore from my strenuous movements. My nocturnal vision was apparently correct, for the brightness grew proportionally to the distance traveled.

Reaching the light, I looked down from a screened vent onto an immense stage surrounded by darkness with a small table and light in the center. Upon the table was an unfinished manuscript whose unbound pages lay scattered in disarray. A sudden impulse made me pass through the vent, climb down to the stage and investigate the nature of this incomplete work. It seemed to be a textbook on mathematical expressions by some obscure professor. The pages were disordered. Some were perhaps missing. Thus the structure was violated. The meaning was out of context. However I did manage to capture the gist of the story. The story?

It was a geometric story about a mathematical progression into infinity. The plot was centered about an algebraic proof. The subject, a mathematical symbol. The given, a variable with a value unknown. The form, by necessity, was the first person narrative. Thus it was as confusing as any subjective account. Nevertheless, picking a page at random, I proceeded to read it as it was.

I was bored. It was getting late and every moment I was growing older. And yet nothing was happening. The time had not yet come. I wanted to leave. I wanted to remove myself from these premises, but I simply could not respond. It was like a dream over which I had no control, for the story had no structure. Fragmented and distorted it seemed to lose all sense of meaning and purpose. It was simply there, as it was, without excuse or justification, to be dealt with and interpreted as one saw fit.

I had to stop this infinite regress before I could no longer resist. I had to stop the progression before it became too late. I left the stage and climbed back into the confining crawl-space. With relief I continued my journey into darkness.

"What was happening?" I wondered as I wandered. I seemed to be following a passage over which I had no control. I was limiting myself to the nether regions of the Structure, and the only way out was to pursue my course to the end. I was compelled forward by necessity, by the inability to turn back, to return to a mock repetition of the past. I must simply press on to what lay ahead.

In the darkness my head bumped against the end of the passage. I pushed open the vent and crawled out onto the plush carpeting of what seemed to be a theater lobby. Excitement filled the air as people moved about or stood talking in small groups. Yet, in all the crowd, no one noticed my unusual emergence. I swung the screen shut, straightened and brushed off my clothes, then wandered about the lobby. It was immense—reaching as far as the eyes could see. Refreshment stands and gift shops were scattered about, contrasting the royal decor. After the isolation outside, the atmosphere was refreshingly filled with life. A sense of unity pervaded the air like that of a group of vacationers on tour.

A marquise above the theater entrance described the show in strangely complex words and symbols. Signs and subtitles covered the board like a sophisticated equation or formula of nature. I began reading the message, but could not pass beyond the first line. The correlation was beyond me. My focus was scattered. Dazed, I pondered over phrases and sub-sections grasping, here and there, subtle meanings and hidden thoughts. Yet I failed to understand the meaning of even one sentence. No sooner had I grasped one concept than I forgot the preceding one so that by the end of the line I was bewildered and lost. Using some strange form of communication, the message seemed to convey subconscious images rather than thoughts.

Restlessness and discontent were all I could feel, and for the first time I questioned my position in life, my goal and my progress, my reason for living. What was I doing here? Why was I stagnating? I grew disillusioned as I glanced at the chronometer. Four-thirty! And I had courses in the morning. But so what. What difference did it make? Yet my desire for sleep returned, and I wandered off through the crowds in search of egress.

I soon came upon a royal stairway with a base of semicircular, red-carpeted stairs. Following them up quickly made me exhausted, for they seemed never-ending. Each time I reached one landing another set of stairs led upward without revealing an exit. I had no choice but to move on unless I was willing to descend.

Eventually I noticed the almost imperceptible change in the decor. Not only had the stairway become narrower, but the plush carpet was now a worn-out rug. Up ahead it vanished altogether, revealing rickety, wooden steps. The beautiful hand-carved balustrade had also decayed into a shabby handrail. Up ahead it disappeared, leaving nothing to grasp. At this height, the steepness and narrowness gave me vertigo. I was almost falling backwards as I dropped to my hands and knees and clambered up the stairs. Disturbed by these nightmarish transformations, I was relieved to find an exit at the top of the next landing. Yet on opening the door I was astonished by the familiar sight. The hallway to my apartment lay before me! In disbelief I closed the door and examined it from a distance. For years I had passed by taking it for a broom or linen closet, yet all along it had led to a vast, subterranean chamber just beneath my room.

I left the doorway and walked back to my apartment, pondering over the strange events of the night. It was like a dream. And yesterday seemed like another world, a world to which I could never return. I entered my room and collapsed on the bed, instantly dropping off into a deep, fitful sleep.

Chapter Three:
VAGABOND OF THE SPIRIT

———————————

Wisdom exists in knowing that life transcends. . . . And so does life.

—IRIS

TOTAL DARKNESS was my solace. For years I wait-ed in oppressive silence, enshrouded by the void as by a cocoon. I endured the metamorphosis in antic-ipation of my emergence. At last the time had come. For countless years we had trained for this moment, undergoing the harsh rigors necessary for survival. We had sacrificed everything. Our lives were noth-ing but the preparation for this one, unique mission, this unprecedented movement into the void. Alien life, such as ourselves, could not begin to anticipate the strange world we were about to enter. Uncharted and unexplored, it challenged us with the unknown. We would be the first organized expedition, the first intelligent race to set eyes upon this world. No one knew what we would find. For the time we lay dor-mant we could only dream of its mysteries. Isolated from one another, each in his separate cell, we were transformed into beings of a different order, and no one doubted that we would emerge more alien to ourselves than to anything else. Yet how could any-one really say? For who among us remembers our life before the void? Indeed, what remains are but scattered dreams and incoherent memories. Were they mere flights of fancy? Who could deny such a possibility? Who was to say that our lives did not begin with the cocoon, that the years of discipline were merely the formula for synthesis and development? The years of seclusion and deprivation could be the natural, nurturing process of the void, a tenderness and care from birth to growth and maturity. Of course it severed us from everything, but who was to say what it would sever us from? Already our increased awareness and sensitivity made us concede the likelihood of self-deception. And as time passed, as the stasis continued, we grew increasingly doubtful of such a former life, for the dreams seemed stranger and wilder, almost impossible. Eventually all of us had no doubt of its illusion, regarding the void as our true birth. Even our mission and purpose seemed inherent, not something contrived with careful planning, but rather a natural instinct. Yet who could explain the happenings in this empty stillness, this impenetrable darkness and silence of the eternal? For having no basis of reference, we were compelled to form our judgments from pure speculation. We ourselves were in such a state of fluctuation and metamorphosis, how could we say what was really true? The transformation was so drastic that even now our forms were radically altered, so alien to our former recollections who could say what version was real? And then again, future development might be completely incompatible with our current state. All we knew was our present form, and even that was growing increasingly compromised.

We rested quietly in our separate cells, carefully evolving and maturing until the time had come when we were complete. We felt it instinctively and simultaneously as though informed by some innate, collective mind. The message came from within.

* * * * *

I opened my eyes to the darkness and silence. Was I supposed to remember something? If so, I didn't know what. It was there, yet I failed to make it materialize. I seemed to have been possessed by an alien from another realm! For the brief period of my dream I was someone or something else, but it wasn't a dream. I was certain of that, for in a dream all things are blurred and unreal. You awake with a full realization. However this time everything but the message was clear and distinct. I remembered each moment of the transposition with precision and concrete reality. I was there. I was actually someone else. I turned on the light and glanced at the time. It was already evening. Having retired so late, I had slept through the day and missed my courses. And yet it made no difference, for I doubted that I would have attended even if awake.

I was plagued with doubt. Was I really myself? Was it possible that I was mutating into another form, an alien form? Or could it be madness? Was exposure beyond the West Walls, however brief, already taking effect? Doubtful of my position, I wandered into the corridor for a change of scene. Although my life was the subject of a complete transformation everything else seemed to have remained the same. People followed the same routine as usual, unaware of any strangeness in my appearance.

Who was I? What was I doing here? What was

I doing anywhere? I remembered nothing of my origins. What little recalled from my past was useless. Incredible as it seems, for all I knew I was simply thrust forth into existence without a reason, for no purpose. I was simply here! And, unreflecting, I had accepted the conditions of this existence without question.

I wandered through the Structure and scanned my past with disgust. That couldn't be me—that ineffectual, mindless creature: conscious, yet without consciousness, a decadent slave to a purposeless existence. The review of that stranger's life was nauseating: living from day to day, willfully taking part in a meaningless absurdity. From the examination of his life came an interrogation of my own. What was the nature of my existence? How had I come to be here? As a rational being it was inconceivable that I had lost these fundamental principles. No wonder the chaos of my present state. To retrieve these principles was my primary concern, for how could I possibly function without them? Helpless in determining the advantageous from the harmful, I had no idea what to do or how to proceed. It was like seeing for the first time. What was it all for? What was the purpose underlying this strange form of existence? Penetrating these mysteries was my first priority in ascertaining my position and reorienting my life.

"I've been looking for you," said a voice sneaking up from behind. I turned to see the eager smile of what appeared to be the Professor's Assistant. But was this some joke? For he was dressed in rags and was panhandling like a bum.

"We're collecting donations for Dreams, Incorporated. Anything you have will be deeply appreciated." It was no joke. I was obviously mistaken in identity. In my pocket I found some change along with a crumpled piece of paper. I gave the tokens to the representative and then glanced at the paper. A chill went down my back, for there in bold letters was one astonishing word: IRIS! The name of the young nurse who brought me to life, the dream image that had sustained me through that terrible night, now had mysteriously appeared before my eyes. Then suddenly, like a returning dream the memory of Katon flashed through my mind. "See her," he had said while handing me the paper, and it was I myself who had placed it in my pocket. "See her," were his instructions, and yet there was no following address. How would I find her if she had no fixed position? Like a rainbow that kept moving ever-farther as one approached.

"Is that all?" enquired the representative, recalling me to the present. I pulled some paper currency from another pocket. I was dumbfounded by the coincidence between Katon and Iris. How had they come to know each other? How had the most important people in my life suddenly become intertwined? "Anything else?" said the voice. I checked my other pockets, shrugged in apology and walked away. The memory of the previous night now flooded my mind. I recalled the dreamlike sequence of events up to the encounter with the indecipherable marquise. I was now determined to return and attend the show. I descended the first flight of stairs and set out in search of the mysterious theater. Who could have guessed that the descent would initiate a nightmare revolution that would inexorably alter my fate?

I wandered down many flights of stairs, past what was surely many levels of the Structure, and yet found no egress, nothing but the continual zigzag of stairs. Eventually I caught sight of the bottom of the staircase, but on moving closer I was alarmed by the unexpected sight of the Sub-Basement. Had I penetrated so deeply? Was I destined to repeat the same course? As I proceeded into the subterranean world the memory of the demonic monster returned. The thought of the encounter set me on guard. And my apprehension was quickly justified, for with the first few steps came a sudden, unprovoked attack.

"Murderer!" screamed someone as I was grabbed and flung to the ground. I was dazed by the attack, but looking up at my assailant brought sudden understanding. A wild-eyed madman stood ready to pounce. However on seeing my face he realized the mistake. "I'm sorry," he whined as he dropped to his knees. His scraggly hair and dirty clothes were certain indications that he was a seasoned explorer. "I'm sorry," he repeated as he broke into tears. My amazement turned to pity as I watched this tragic monstrosity fall apart. "I'm sorry," he cried, and suddenly his words were no longer directed to me, but to something much deeper, something much more tragic. "I thought you were someone else," he explained, and then he went into some gibberish about cocoons and butterflies and how they flew away and would never again be seen. "The others," he began, and the remembrance twisted his face with pain, "they tortured the caterpillars!" The memory was propelling him forward, gaining momentum as it drove him back into the past. "Swarms of ants. Piercing! Tearing! Searing pain! Devoured alive in slow, agonizing death!" He paused for a moment, his breathing fast and heavy, his eyes in a trance, lost in another world.

"She asked me up for hot chocolate," he murmured to himself, and his childlike reverie brought calmness and nostalgia to his eyes. "My teacher, Miss Iris, the pretty lady who saw me sitting all alone in the cold." With this pleasant reflection came tranquility to his soul. He proceeded calmly as though nothing had happened.

* * * * *

"I have to ask my parents," said the little boy, for he was just a child at the time.

"Of course," Miss Iris smiled.

Having gained permission he entered her home, followed her up a dark staircase, through her living room, and out onto the balcony porch. She leaned against the black, iron railing and pointed down to where she had seen him sitting.

"I saw you from up here," she said with a smile. He looked down and saw himself playing with the water in the gutter. "Time passes slowly when there's nothing to do."

Iris explained her hobby of protecting butterflies, showing him her glass asylum of cocoons. To preserve them from predators hundreds were gathered in jars on the balcony porch. They were collected during the fall, sheltered from the harsh winter, and stored safely till the arrival of spring. She was their unknown guardian and their assurance of survival. She described their transformation with picturesque clarity, conjuring in his mind intricate patterns of color and movement. A fascination for the delicate beauty and a longing to witness their miraculous appearance made him anticipate the moment when they would emerge from their living tombs and fly away.

* * * * *

"They're gone!" he suddenly screamed. His outburst sent a jolt of adrenalin through my veins. "They've vanished," he whimpered. "The Structure has won." He collapsed in despair, his eyes closing as he succumbed to exhaustion and sleep. But his soul would not rest, for while drifting off he mumbled something about demons pursuing him through the night.

"Don't worry," I whispered to ease his fears. "I'll be here. No one will harm you." I sat quietly in contemplation, keeping watch over this miserable tragedy of a man, baby-sitting this Structural outcast as though he were a child. Considering his lamentable condition I had no doubt that he had traveled far beyond the West Walls, for nothing else could generate such turmoil and terror. Nothing else could explain the madness of his mind. But what was it he had seen? What nightmare could have driven him to such despair? What memory was responsible for his tormented soul? Our worlds were converging. Somehow everything was connecting with some pivotal source. Katon, Iris, the Professor, the Theater, the dreams, and now even the Madman himself— each was a clue to unraveling the mystery. The Madman was obviously my closest link. He was, after all, right before me, and he was going nowhere. If only he could reveal the secret of his insanity. I resolved to wait and ferret out this knowledge. And thus I sat back in weariness, impatiently considering the all-night vigil.

A sudden flickering of the lights jarred me from my seat! Fearful of blindness and darkness I stood frozen to the spot. My heart began pounding as I anticipated the power failure.

"Wake up," I called, but the Madman didn't stir. The dimming lights flickered out. I was abandoned in the total darkness of the Sub-Basement. With the pitch blackness came an ominous feeling of doom, a danger perhaps lurking only one step away, only one step away from death. No wonder people went mad. And now my nightmares returned. Rumors of demons sent an iciness trembling through my veins. With the sudden stillness in the air, a terrifying moment by moment anticipation of horror, I realized that they were already here.

"Wake up," I whispered as I reached down to the Madman. But my hand passed through empty space. I became frantic. The piercing scream that shattered the silence I soon realized was my own. The answering echo down the corridor would have been less unnerving had it been my own. But it was laughter, not a scream, an insane, demonic laughter which gathered momentum as it converged and overwhelmed.

I scrambled up the stairs, driven through the darkness by my impending doom. It seemed forever before I would emerge from the dark, but the lighted passage of the upper levels shone like a beacon, signaling my approach to comfort and safety. Eventually I reached the light and familiar surroundings, yet the sight of civilization was no calmative, for the nightmare image held fast, goading me with the promise of death or insanity. I had no idea where I was running. All that mattered was to move as far as possible from my horror. Hour after hour I ran without stopping, through lobbies and corridors, past people who eyed me with curiosity and suspicion. Drained of energy, disoriented by the flight, I eventually found my way to public lodgings, entered the large dormitory and collapsed on the nearest cot. Through weakness and exhaustion I soon lost my fear. Feeling safe among the crowd, some sleeping, others talking quietly, I allowed myself, not really to fall asleep, but rather to succumb to a state of voluntary unconsciousness.

* * * * *

"Destination?" asked someone. I glanced over to the clerk seated at a desk.

"Destination?" I queried, dumbfounded.

"Current destination?" he repeated in a bored, bureaucratic tone. I scanned the surroundings to make sure there was no mistake, perhaps someone else he was addressing. I then noticed with dismay the darkness of the immense stage.

"Destination for what?" I asked. "What are you talking about?"

"Your present destination?" he enquired while flipping casually through some pamphlets. "Where is it you're going?"

"Going!" I exclaimed. "I'm not going anywhere."

"Then what are you doing here?" he asked in surprise.

"I'm not sure," I responded in helpless confusion. "I don't even know where I am."

"Try and remember. You must have had some reason for coming here."

"I don't know," I confessed. "Everything's blank. I can't recall where I came from or even how I got here."

"Let me get this straight," the clerk continued while taking down notes. "You don't know where you are, where you came from, or where you're going. Let's see your identity papers."

"I have none," I explained after quickly checking my pockets. "I have never had any." But on closer inspection I found a small, crumpled piece of paper with the letters, I R I S, printed in bold type.

"What's that?" he demanded.

"I don't know. I can't remember." I offered him the paper.

"Iris," he said decisively. "That's who you are." But it didn't ring a bell. He then pulled out a reference book entitled The Revolutionary Dictionary. After thumbing the pages he stopped and began reading the definition. "Iris: 1. A circular membrane encompassing the pupil of the eye. 2. A rainbow. 3. An alien sorceress of dreams in science-fiction mythology. 4. A prismatic display of color. 5. A plant and any of its variously colored flowers. 6. Goddess of the rainbow. Messenger of the gods." He eyed me suspiciously and asked if I were any of these. I denied the inference and told him he was an idiot.

"Loss of identity," the idiot repeated slowly as he wrote.

"But I'm not Iris," I argued. "This paper isn't mine. I have no idea who or what Iris is nor how this paper came into my possession. I don't have any identity papers now nor have I ever before."

"No identity papers," he transcribed as he spoke. "Subject claims a case of mistaken identity." But as I glanced down I noticed that the clerk was filing a missing person's report. "No idea why he is here," he continued, "nor what he is doing. Tell me," he added with a scrutinizing glare, "how did you get here?"

"I don't even know where here is," I answered with embarrassment. "Suddenly I was here," I added in apology.

"Oh come now," he remarked as though offended, "do you take me for a fool?"

"No, only an idiot," I thought to myself.

Receiving no response he shrugged his shoulders and resumed writing. "Suddenly he's here. That's a good one," he laughed. "No explanation," he added in conclusion. Then suddenly a moment's inspiration flashed over his face. "Are you mad?" he asked, rising to his feet and leaning across the desk. "Have you been beyond the West Walls?" There was silence and stillness. The question reverberated through my mind as the scene faded into darkness.

* * * * *

To my relief I found myself lying within the darkness of my room. Then suddenly, jolted to my senses, I realized that instead of here, I should be awakening miles away in public lodgings! The clerk's suspicion of madness now seemed insightful, for how else could the discrepancy be explained? Unless it was all a dream. Yet my nocturnal journey seemed too horrifyingly real. It couldn't be a dream. Only one course of action could resolve the dilemma. I left the room and started off down the corridor, retracing the dream flight of the previous night. Yet even if I succeeded, even if there were such a journey, it still could not account for my bodily displacement. A successful investigation would only affirm my dementia. If an overpowering urge had not lured me forward, my timidity would have turned me back, conceding it as all a form of delirium.

As I pressed farther through the Structure I was unnerved by my ability to negotiate unfamiliar passages. Still I traveled on, searching for the end of my journey, the public lodging. These lodgings were invaluable to those on the move. At any time, at any place, one could stop in and rest. Available to everyone, they were the scene of traveling artists, students, musicians, and poets, not to mention the vagabonds, bums, mentally disabled, and the elderly. All of them had one thing in common—a desire for rest. The lodgings not only provided shelter, but also a feeling of camaraderie in the unknown. It was one of the few redeeming qualities of the Structure. But ironically enough, the Structure was being undermined by this continual free-flow of movement, for the underground flourished through the premises of public lodgings. Revolutionists, madmen, criminals, and outcasts—all merged with and traveled indistinguishably from the crowd. There was no telling them apart. Nevertheless, the lodgings were a definite haven for those in transit. Their support basis was surprisingly unknown.

Finally, after hours of walking, I stood outside the public lodgings of my dream, yet here it was in everyday reality. Or was this reality? The uncanniness of the moment captured my being. Why was this happening? Why was it happening to me, of all people? Dazed through loss of reason, unable to accept the collapse of conventional reality, I was compelled forward through an almost independent force from within. In somnambulistic trance I re-entered the nightmare, walking slowly across the room to where I had slept. An old man was lying upon my cot with an open book covering his face. Curious as to its content, and also to obtain a better view of his face, an irresistible impulse and an impetuousness foreign to my unassuming nature forced me to act. Carefully, almost unwillingly, I gently removed the book so as not to disturb the soundness of his sleep.

"He's dead!" exclaimed a voice in horror. The whole room sprang to their feet and crowded around the bed. "He murdered him!" shouted an old man pointing his finger in accusation. "I saw him do it!" I was shocked, unable to say a word in defense. I could do nothing but gaze at the ghastly corpse. In the eyes of the crowd, my silence only confirmed my guilt. I tried to speak, to deny the accusation, but some nightmarish force withheld the words. Then suddenly, breaking the tension, came a voice to my rescue.

"He's innocent," she said as she stepped forward from the crowd. "Why, he's only a child." I couldn't believe it. Was it Iris? After all the dreams and doubts could she be real?

"He's as old as any of you," claimed the old man. "He murdered him and then he stole his book."

"It's mine!" I cried, finally breaking the spell and regaining control. He lunged to grab it away, but I clutched the book and broke through the crowd, rushing from the room and down the corridor.

"Stop him!" yelled the old man. "He's a Revolutionist! Don't let him escape!—Guards!" he screamed as I ran through the hall. Alarms rang throughout the Structure.

I regretted leaving Iris, but I was compelled by necessity to run for my life. My flight was carrying me farther from home, but it made no difference, for I realized that I would never be able to return. My courses, my colleagues, my entire life was now a thing of the past, for I had become a fugitive of the Structure, something I had once despised.

After running for some time, and confident that no one was following, I relaxed into a leisurely pace to avoid suspicion. I glanced at the book and only now recognized its title: The Time Has Come, by Katon! The realization brought me to a standstill. After all the searching and doubting, after all the useless speculation the book was now in my hands. Just as Iris had come to life, so the dream had also come true. I found a secluded spot and nestled down to read.

I opened my treasure and strained to make out

the words in the darkness of the corner alcove. The only light filtered in from off the main corridor, keeping me hidden, but unable to see. Angling the book toward the source of light, I barely made out the wording of the title page: The Time Has Come: An Account of Experiences Beyond the West Walls, by Katon, Revolutionary Press Unlimited, a subsidiary of Dreams, Incorporated. What struck me was the absence of a publishing date, for previous considerations evoked the question of whether The Time Has Come was old or new. Possible explanations were that an ancient book may never have been recorded. While, on the other hand, a recent book may not have yet been recognized. Without a date the only clue was the style of typography. The letters were shaped strangely as though from a different language and time, yet however difficult to recognize, they were essentially the same as the modern form. My eyes were adjusting to the darkness and so I proceeded to the next page and read:

> For countless years I followed his path, pursuing him through a thousand lands. But time after time he eluded the search, vanishing just beyond my reach, escaping every possible attempt. Constant failure took its toll. Eventually I became an aging man, laboring to maintain even the most casual pursuit, yet held by the vision of my only goal. Breathless, but running, refusing to rest, I disdained whatever slowed my pace. Struggling after him, finally I closed in, determined not to allow him escape. Our

footsteps echoed throughout the empty passage. Then suddenly, stopping and turning, he spoke calmly with curiosity. "Yes?" he asked as though only now realizing that I was following. Stunned and at a loss for words I stood helplessly like a fool incapable of knowing what to do, realizing only now the senseless nature of the pursuit.

Commotion erupted down the main corridor. Guards were coming. Unlike the character in the story, they knew what they were after and what they would do when they found me—and so did I. I postponed *The Time Has Come* and rose to my feet. I made sure the coast was clear before continuing my journey, moving deeper into unfamiliar regions of the Structure.

After playing an all day game of cat-and-mouse with the guards I found my way to public lodgings for the night. I realized that I must disguise myself so as not to be recognized. How? I was uncertain, but each moment I delayed was a moment closer to capture. I sat down upon a cot, opened the book, not really intending to read, I was too exhausted for that, but simply to marvel at my long-sought treasure. I pondered my situation. Only a few days ago my life had been so concrete and direct. I had felt secure and at home in the world of the Structure. But recently everything had become confused and momentous. Hardly was I able to rest in one place before being thrust forth into new surroundings and novel situations, and now that I was a fugitive criminal it would remain so forever. From now on would be constant running and hiding. There was no longer any home or respite for this eternal wanderer and vagabond of the spirit.

Lying back upon the cot, my tension and exhaustion gradually waned, but the light kept me awake even through closed eyes. Without thinking I placed the open book upon my face to shield the light as well as my identity. It suddenly dawned on me that this is how I had found the old man—the dead man. Would I also wake up dead? But my worries and confusion vanished slowly, losing their grip as I released my hold and succumbed to the inner world of my dream.

Chapter Four:
SUBLIMINAL PROJECTIONS

That which moves quickly is seen only with a discerning eye.

—IRIS

I EMERGED into cold, blinding whiteness. With half-closed eyes I stumbled through a thick, powdery substance into some shade. Something had gone wrong. Our mission had been compromised. I shivered from the cold. My eyes were squinting, blinking, and half-bedazzled. Slowly they grew accustomed to the glare and I hesitantly looked up into the brilliant whiteness of the strange, new world.

A miscalculation had occurred in either the timing or the placement, for the world was nothing but a frozen wasteland. An endless expanse of white powder flowed and merged unimpeded with the horizon. Fortunately, being placed on high ground, I was able to scan and locate the focal point with ease. I triangulated my directions with the source of light and proceeded to traverse the shortest distance to the point. However, as I trudged off through the field of powder my coordinated movement soon became slow and exhausting. Therefore I was surprised on finding myself the first to rendezvous.

I waited patiently, fully exposed to the alien environment. As time passed and no others arrived I grew certain that the suspected mishap had occurred, that our mission was now doomed from the start to failure. Then suddenly it struck me: perhaps it was I who had failed. Perhaps I had come too late. Perhaps they had already rendezvoused and left, leaving me behind and all alone in this alien world. What was I to do? What could I do? But eventually my fears dissolved on spotting a black form moving closer from off the horizon. I felt empowered as he drew near, for we were a unity of being, capable of surviving only in relation to each other. With his approach came hope, for even were we the only survivors there was still a possibility for success. I calmly anticipated his difficult progression. Finally, through total exertion, he reached the focal point in an exhausted, yet self-disciplined state of being. We stood at attention, patiently awaiting the arrival of others, in stoic defiance of the freezing cold.

Eventually we noticed their approach, some from the hills, others moving up from the valley, their black uniforms in marked contrast to the white landscape. They were the only motion in the emptiness of this frozen world. One by one they rendezvoused, waiting silently at attention for all to gather. With each arrival our force magnified. The circle increased in numbers as more black figures struggled their way through the powder, filtering in from every direction. None would have guessed that from above, our rendezvous took on a frightful appearance. There in a lifeless desert of pure white an ominous blackness was growing in size and power. And yet none could have failed to notice the silent beauty of the rendezvous: a black flower blossoming—a center of black alternating with concentric rings of white and black surrounded and interpenetrated by radiating rays or paths across the otherwise unbroken white, powdered crust.

Finally we had coalesced. The Field Marshal, who was the last to arrive, stepped forward into the center of the formation. As he circled about, his eyes rested upon the countenance of each member. His penetrating gaze pierced their souls, discerning their essence, confronting an equally powerful magnitude of force. Satisfied that all were present, a slight nod was all that was necessary to send several of our party into the vast, uncharted region to the west. The scouts were the forerunners and guides of the expedition. To work effectively they needed to alienate themselves from the others. They were destined by necessity to travel alone. With another slight nod from the Field Marshal the remaining members broke formation and set out to examine the hitherto unknown aspects of this world. After a few moments the first discovery was made by one of the younger, inexperienced members of the group.

"They're crystals," he announced as he knelt upon the ground. "The land is covered with a layer of small, white crystals free for the taking." Everyone dropped to the ground and scooped up a handful of the cold powder. They were indeed tiny, perfectly formed crystals of which no two seemed alike. Each had a pattern of perfection all its own, a beauty and a unique essence inconsistent with this barren world. Yet something was wrong. Slowly the darkness converged. Slowly the awakening unfolded as the scene faded into memory.

"It's melting," whispered a voice from my dream. For a moment at least, I could still feel their presence as their words held me back.

"They're fading away," said another with disappointment. "They're ephemeral. They don't last." And in a moment they had vanished as I opened my eyes to the common sight of public lodgings.

My mind had been possessed. What else could explain my psychic transposition? What else could explain my fascination for common snow? I had lost my identity and been immersed in an alien soul. No simple dream could be the source of such a dynamic exchange. There must be something more, for the experience was as real as anything in life. And to my astonishment I wondered—perhaps more real than life. I had no doubt of the reality of the expedition. No matter what others would say I knew that it was true and that somewhere, even now, the alien exploration was still taking place.

How odd it seemed that what was clearly a dream appeared so authentic, so much more meaningful than real life, whereas real life had, on the other hand, mutated so completely into a nightmare. My whole world had collapsed, casting me out as a homeless wanderer without direction, without hope of return. Now that the past had been crushed what was there left for me to do? Being a fugitive of the Structure what else could I do but run? And yet I had nowhere to go, nothing left but the emptiness of total freedom, a myriad of choice and chance.

But there was something. An equally strange dream world was haunting me with its elusiveness. The tentative world of Iris, Katon, and the Professor, with their fleeting moments of reality—here one instant, gone the next, their intangible presence whimsically sustained as the visions of a dream. I had no idea where they were nor how to reach them. They seemed to come and go of their own volition without any prior warning or indication. Chance encounters were simply a coincidence of time and place rather than design and intent. For this reason I involuntarily succumbed to scanning the world for their presence. Whether in hallways or crowded assemblies I was unable to resist scrutinizing each person for the faintest resemblance. Even the slightest possibility was enough to set me wondering whether it was one of my elusive comrades.

Sometimes in lecture halls and auditoriums I would spend hours observing the backs of people's heads or profiles, watching their every movement and gesture, hoping till the very end that they've come only to find with a slight turn of the head the most shockingly asinine face in the world. There was no use to it all. They came when they came, and nothing more could be done. Yet one hope still remained, perhaps the book—and then suddenly it struck me. It was gone! Katon's book was gone! My lifelong treasure had vanished overnight. Had it been stolen? I collapsed on the bed and tried calming myself. After a few moments I concluded that it must be somewhere within the premises, for books simply don't disappear. Some curious reader must have retrieved it from off the floor and nestled down with it for the night. Quietly, so as not to disturb the early morning hours of their sleep, I moved slowly around the room scanning everyone's possessions for The Time Has Come. Imagine my surprise on finding someone, who for a moment I had taken to be

Iris, smiling up at me from her bed.

"What is it?" she asked with a touch of mockery. "Do you enjoy studying people while they sleep?" She had obviously awakened earlier than I, and had found my strange antics entertaining.

"I'm looking for The Time Has Come," I explained in confusion, unable to decide whether or not it was really she.

"Well the time has come, so go ahead and look," she said with amusement. And that was just what I did. I could do nothing but puzzle over her familiar appearance. She seemed identical to Iris, and yet her hair was of a different style and of a darker color. Unless Iris had changed her hair overnight it was impossible that they were one, yet the possibility, however slight, nevertheless remained. I resumed the search, but the enigma forced me to glance back at her sly, smiling face. Either this was a naturally friendly woman or else Iris was playing a game and enjoying it immensely.

The search was fruitless. Unless the book was hidden, it was no longer here. Unable to search further into their belongings I resolved to continue on my way and accept the loss. I moved to the doorway and turned to catch the eye and smile of the only one awake.

"Where are you going?" she whispered in consternation. Not wishing to disturb the silence I simply shrugged my shoulders. "Is something wrong?" she asked as she came to the door. "Are you in some trouble?" I could not lie even though I realized the unlikelihood of her being Iris.

"I'm a criminal," I replied. "I'm wanted for murder." This answer had no effect, for she seemed unperturbed.

"I know a place," she suggested. "They'll give you asylum. You'll be safe." She quickly gathered her possessions and returned to my side. "Come on," she urged, pulling me by the arm, "let's go somewhere where we can talk in privacy." She led the way through corridors and lobbies, taking me on some unknown journey to which I had not the slightest reason to object, for I had nowhere else to go, no other hope of escape. And though I could never be certain, her concern was unlike that of a stranger. Therefore I submitted to her guidance in hopes that she was indeed Iris.

"Who are you?" I asked, no longer able to bear the suspense.

"Who am I?" she repeated in surprise. "Why what difference does it make? I am whatever I am," she replied in a light, joyous manner. "No name is needed for that, for I am constantly changing, eternally becoming. I am the formless as well as the concrete. I am by nature and profession," and here she paused for dramatic effect, "an actress." With this she delightfully took my hand and we continued, arm in arm, to our destination.

"What's this?" I enquired, glancing at the hand I held. On her finger was a beautiful, blue crystal ring which glowed and sparkled like a dancing fire. "Are you married?" I asked while at the same time dreading her response.

"Not in the way you think," she replied with amusement in her eyes.

We traveled the remainder of the day in silence,

stopping now and then for refreshments and rest. There was very little to say, very little that needed saying, for as time passed we grew increasingly closer. Nothing could explain this sudden affinity with one another, this empathic delight in understanding and oneness. It was almost as though I had known her all my life, as though we were together in some past incarnation, a childhood dream long forgotten.

Though her appearance had changed I was certain she was Iris, for nothing else could explain our intimacy. Deep within her crystal-blue eyes the secret shone though the masks and illusions. As she led the way to asylum I asked if she had ever heard of a hospital called "Dreams, Incorporated."

She laughed in surprise. "That's no hospital. It's a theatrical company. It's the acting agency for which I work. Wherever did you get the idea it was a hospital?"

At least now it was out. No matter how confusing the interpretation, at least she had acknowledged her affiliation with the enterprise. But even her admission proved nothing but the mere existence of Dreams, Incorporated. It neither clarified the situation, nor revealed her true identity. Would I ever know the truth? I realized only now, that what she had said was true. What difference did it make who she was? That she was simply herself was all that mattered.

"Since you mentioned it," she suggested, "the theater isn't far. If you want, you can see our current productions." I agreed, not merely out of curiosity and intrigue, but also out of sheer exhaustion. For anything, any sort of diversion would be a welcome change from our seemingly endless journey. And so once again she led the way. "It's getting dark," she added. "They'll be starting soon."

To my astonishment we arrived at the strange, majestic theater—the theater from the night of the Professor's lecture, the night of Katon and of the West Walls. Had I simply traveled in circles? Was it all the same course? And yet the movement seemed novel. Once again the feeling of tourism returned through the noise and excitement, the laughter, the anticipation, but most of all through the sense of unity in sharing a special event. We wandered through the crowded lobby, passing small gift shops, stopping now and then before a curious display. Eventually we worked our way to the main entrance. The incessant din of the crowd muffled all sounds, and even as she shouted I had to lean forward to distinguish her words.

"It's already started!" she exclaimed, pointing up at the sign covered with strange words and symbols. The marquise had apparently been altered, the patterns changed, the symbols rewritten or replaced, nevertheless the message had remained the same: indecipherable. And yet it would soon forge my fate.

We entered the theater with a sense of wonder and adventure. Its vastness engendered the vagueness of omnipresence, for with limitless extension, with a continual series of alcoves and small, out-of-the-way sub-theaters, its scope was magnified beyond imagination. In the darkness we wound our way through a maze of auditoriums. Partitions, both temporary and permanent, were strewn about, forming small, separate nooks for less popular programs.

The haphazard arrangement of the theater suggested an offhand construction, an almost whimsical and ever-changing design. The discontinuity was evident most strikingly in the small viewing screens placed at random intervals along the walls of the larger theaters. Around them, people gathered, both standing and sitting in all types of chairs: folding chairs, lounge chairs, stools and boxes, anything available was put to use. But most curious of all was the disconcerting atmosphere of noise and confusion. Simultaneous programs performed in the same area went unnoticed by each group of viewers who seemed absorbed in their own little show.

We cleared a path through the crowds of people and chairs, pressing deeper into the mysterious darkness of the theater. The disordered atmosphere, with the distraction of sideline conversations and spectators who roamed about, coming and going as they pleased, produced a chaos which nevertheless had no adverse effect upon the presentation of any show.

Eventually, as would be expected, my companion and I became separated by the darkness. Rushing frantically around, spurred by the sense of aloneness and loss, I searched everywhere. Retracing our path and exploring every possible avenue came to nothing. I would have called her name, but since I wasn't sure, I could only scan the auditorium for her presence. On spotting her vague resemblance in the distance I hurried over to the uncertain prospect only to find disappointment. Eventually logic and a sense of helplessness persuaded me to backtrack to the point of separation and await her return.

I lounged back in an old recliner. This may take some time, maybe even a lifetime. Carefully I observed the continual flux of changing faces until the boredom of my wake, along with the strangely alluring program on the main screen diverted my attention. Its mesmeric powers evoked an instinctive aversion within my soul. Yet however much I fought to free myself, however much I fought against its controlling influence, my independence of will finally succumbed to its seduction. Sinking back comfortably in the chair brought a release and absorption into the continuous flow of colors and sounds.

Chapter Five:
SURROGATE OF TRUTH

———————————

The greatest actors are those who think the play is real.

—IRIS?

"IT'S CHRISTMAS!" she sang delightfully as they entered the crowded department store. Last minute shoppers were rushing about, selecting that hard to determine "just right" present. Rainbow lights and fanciful decorations spiced up the Yuletide spirit. Familiar carols rekindled the childhood dreams and pleasant memories of this special season. Multi-colored lights blinked on and off. Beautiful ornaments draped the trees and displays, enhancing the fairyland atmosphere. Ethereal angels danced to music. Elves and fairies built toys, wrapped gifts, and baked cakes and cookies. Reindeer pranced in place while pulling Santa's sleigh. And it was snowing! Despite forecasts to the contrary this would be the longed-for white Christmas. All these feelings converged to produce her exuberant release of happiness as they moved from the wintry freeze into the warmth and comfort of the crowded store. He encircled her with his arm and soul as they wandered through the congested aisles. It would be their first Christmas together, the most memorable Christmas of all.

How lucky he was to have such a woman for a wife. How often he wondered how it ever came about, for she was a dream come true, a joyous surrender to life. All life long he had been deprived of his soul-mate. All life long he had dreamed of his true love, waiting impatiently for the day their fates would meet, longing for the paradise their love would bring. As a child he had envied those with girlfriends. Their security and comfort in being together intensified his loneliness and desire. Their carefree happiness was a painful mockery of his solitude. How he would treasure her if only they would meet. How he would sacrifice and devote himself to her life, protecting her from the cruel, indifferent world. And so he built up dream upon dream, fashioning her existence from his own ideals. She was his savior, the one person who could bring meaning and fulfillment to his life. She was the missing link necessary to change him from child to man, the link necessary in raising him to the adult world.

But she never came. Year after year he waited in loneliness, dreaming of the fantasy where they would be king and queen. His imagination transformed the commonplace into the fairy-tale setting for their love. His every action was taken to ensure their future. He planned his career, anticipated their life, their home, their family, their love, but nothing ever came about. He eventually resigned himself to solitude. Then one day, like a dream come true, she appeared before his eyes, transforming his mundane existence into a wonderland of delight. The old adage was true: trying too hard can chase away what you desire. Ironically, by surrendering his pursuit, his future had willingly come to him.

How joyful the world now seemed to them. It was as if God or Fate had bestowed some divine favor, as though the universe itself were smiling upon their love. Reflecting over their dismal past, a past of loneliness and sorrow, of seemingly senseless pain and effort they now realized that it had all been justified. They marveled at the childish simplicity of life, having faith that in the end everything would turn out right. The world was now a playground for their amusement, a fantasy realm to enact their own dreams. They were like children reveling in a world of their making. They could do anything, be anything, transforming the world into a mirror of their ideals. Life was a paradise. For they did not hesitate to see the world in such an imaginary light, and with their love fulfilled they could ask for no more.

They separated as she wandered across the aisle for her own shopping. The tune of his favorite Christmas carol played above the clamor of the crowd. The reminiscent music evoked a carefree joy within his soul, and at that moment he was the happiest person in the world. He listened to the holiday music while he browsed along, enlivened by the warmth of the Christmas spirit.

While glancing over the merchandise his eye suddenly chanced upon a crystalline paperweight filled with water. Shaking it in his hand created a raging snowstorm inside the miniature scenery. He watched with amusement as the flakes settled to form a soft, tranquil layer of snow, then shook the crystal bubble again and again each time as the scene grew calm. He had no idea why it appeared so fascinating. His eyes seemed entranced by the childish spectacle. Unable to resist, he shook the bubble again and again, and as much as he tried he couldn't pull himself away. A growing uneasiness soon turned to fear as he remained frozen to the spot, hopelessly enraptured by its spell. A sudden chill swept through his body as he shook the crystal bubble over and over, faster and faster till the snow was one blurred mass of white, and yet still he shook the globe as the swirling cloud drew him closer into its depth, smothering him in a whirlwind of madness.

* * * * *

"We can't stay!" cried a voice out of the blizzard. From the turbulent depths emerged a dark figure which struggled its way to clarity.

"Which way do we go?" I shouted back as he approached, but the moment it was uttered the question faded into the distance, swallowed up and carried off by the sheer force of the wind.

"Anywhere, but we have to move on!" the Field Marshal shouted through the deafening roar. "We'll die if we remain!"

The expedition had taken refuge in a rocky cul-de-sac. Yet it was obvious that we could no longer remain, for even though sheltered from the full brunt of the storm, the icy air was still penetrating our uniforms, sapping us of warmth and energy. Standing our ground meant perishing. Those squatting or sitting already had difficulty rising to their feet. And, incredibly, others had even fallen asleep in the snow. We had to shake them violently in order to rouse them to consciousness. It was imperative to keep moving, for stagnation meant a slow, unconscious death.

The expedition reluctantly assembled its ranks

and proceeded against the onslaught of the storm. We all realized our doom. Our mission was now a certain failure, yet the only alternative to passive death was to move on in hopes of finding shelter. As unlikely as that hope might be it did not hinder our valiant efforts, for we were the last expedition, the sole remaining hope for our people.

We fought our way through the blizzard, struggling with each step against the full force of the elements, forging a path through the wind and snow. Nothing in the world could alter our designated course, and nothing short of death could stop us from reaching our destination. We were aliens perishing in an unknown world, and there was no way for any of us ever to return. There was no way that anyone could possibly help, for we were stranded on a cold, deserted planet, an isolated planet far out in space. With no hope of rescue, and with only the vague notion of some distant goal, we realized that soon we would all be dead. The countless years of preparation were of no avail, for with the sudden whimsical turn of events our lives were rendered meaningless. A chance mishap, an unpredicted storm, such trifling annoyances would foil years of careful planning. The long, painful journey to this world would end in disaster. The dedicated efforts, the hopes and aspirations, the trials and ordeals were all in vain. With fatalistic acceptance of our death, and with a numb and passive acknowledgment of our failure, the expedition pressed on stoically into the freezing storm.

Eventually the inevitable occurred, and it was a miracle that it had not happened sooner. Overcome with exhaustion one of the dark figures suddenly dropped from formation, collapsing upon the snow-covered ground. The expedition silently maintained its position. The travelers watched solemnly as the Field Marshal struggled through the wind and snow over to where the straggler had fallen. It was the youngest, most inexperienced who had fallen first.

"I can't move my legs!" he called out. "I'm numb all over!"

No one needed to explain or justify what had to be done, for there was no possible way to carry him across miles of snowdrift through a raging storm. Each of us could barely make it on his own, and each of us was himself, at any moment, ready to succumb. If we reached safety in time we would send back help, but as it was, we all realized that it was only a matter of time before we too would be left behind. There was no need for words of comfort. Even the straggler knew that his time had come.

"Don't sleep!" the Field Marshal called out as we departed. "No matter how hard it is don't ever succumb! Fight it to the end!"

We left him lying upon the frozen layer of snow. The expedition gathered its courage and marched forward into the full force of the gale. No one dared glance back to see the bewildered expression of his gaze. Already his powers were losing their grasp. Already the storm was covering him with a layer of fine, powdered snow—the snow crystals he himself had discovered with such joy.

The Field Marshal's words apparently had no effect, for merciful sleep soon clouded his mind. With weary eyes he watched from above as the expedition moved slowly over the snow-covered plain—a formation of black arrows drifting across a field of white, pointing the way to some distant goal. Perhaps the mission had been a failure. Perhaps death and destruction had been our fate, but for an instant before losing consciousness, in a momentary glimpse in his twilight state the straggler realized the meaning of our adventure. But as drowsiness overwhelmed him, the sudden insight faded, lost forever in the darkness of the unknown. The straggler was told not to sleep, and yet he did sleep. His eyes and ears closed out the presence of the storm, and he dreamt a dream of another life, a life where this world was no longer real.

* * * * *

The dying sun sank slowly beneath the horizon, casting rays of mellow light and long, dark shadows over the hills and valleys. He sat atop the balcony porch gazing out over the peaceful mountain retreat, gazing out into the melancholy nightfall. Now and then a dog would bark. A child's voice would call out in play. The aroma of Sunday's dinner drifting between the houses, the clang of pots and pans, the ever-fading, ever-darkening sunglow upon the clouds, all merged to evoke the same Sunday blues that had haunted him all through his past. It was a sadness of endings, the passing of one more weekend, the close of one more respite from a life of endless work. What was it all for? Why was he so tired of living? He questioned his way of life to discover the cause of his distress, yet all he knew was that life seemed to have lost its flavor. Existence no longer seemed a challenge. The future no longer held hopes and desires, longing and anticipation, for now, with his goals accomplished the world had nothing more to offer. Life had lost its sense of chance and uncertainty. With security and a predestined future, living had become a boring way to pass the time.

Looking back over the past he found nothing but foolishness and a childishly predictable simplicity. What was the significance of his life? What was it he had really accomplished? He had done what he wanted. He had done what society and even his very nature had expected. He was raising a family and leading a well-adjusted, normal life. Having a son and daughter, a loving wife, a nice home, and a good secure job, he was far better off than most people in the world, and yet something was still missing. Something vague and intangible was lacking. It all seemed so futile. Was this all there was to life? Would he live and die just as billions had lived and died since the dawn of time? He cringed at the thought of such a vulgar fate. There had to be something more to it all. And yet, as he surveyed the totality of life, the sum of all possible courses and actions he realized that it was all a game, a senseless game without meaning or purpose. It was a simple, stimulus-response mechanism of struggle and survival, a fundamentally unconscious drive that ruled the world. Whether it was on the physical, psychological, or even the intellectual and spiritual plane the conditions were always the same—nothing but a predictable causal network was responsible for all motives and actions. There was no such quality as free will.

With apprehension he examined his past and painfully recognized his own foolishness, the pre-designed games in which he himself was a willing participant. He winced shamefully as he remembered all the frustration in longing for his special soul-mate, a loved one to call his own, to protect and to cherish, someone who in return would reciprocate his affection, would consider him the most important person in her life. He sadly realized that love, the one saving hope for mankind, the praised and sacred emotion that symbolized unity and meaning, was nothing but a biologically induced psycho-physical phenomenon.

Looking back over his life he was repulsed by its vanity, how he had striven for the admiration of his peers, how he had vied so desperately for recognition and achievement. It was his own way of influencing others. But he soon realized that this drive was common to everyone, for everyone secretly desired such power and self-esteem. Whether it was the desire to be singled out and respected or the desire to be singled out and rejected, whether it was a desire to stand apart or a desire to blend in, whether to feel oneself good or to feel oneself bad, whether to feel with it or to feel above it, the results were the same. Within everyone, even the wallflower or lone wolf, was the hidden need to feel special or important, somehow acceptable to someone or something. It was the only feeling that could sustain one through such an indifferent world.

Looking now at his contemporaries, he recognized the same patterns of behavior, the struggle for recognition, power, and dominance. Nothing had changed. If anything the situation was worse, for the harmless games, the secret drives and desires were now manifested in more deadly, far more real and dangerous games. He realized with dismay that what he had suspected was true: the world was controlled by children in adult bodies, children who were slaves to their own transitory feelings, children who had not yet matured into autonomous, rational beings, but puppets to every subconscious whim and command. And yet, what difference did it make, for life itself seemed to be in error. Everywhere there was only senselessness and absurdity. Everywhere there was only a monotonous void. As he viewed the life of man he was dismayed by its similarity to the lives of animals. For just as animals, we live from day to day working ceaselessly for food and shelter. We return home to eat and sleep. We search for a mate to produce offspring. We raise our families. We grow old and die. And the cycle repeats with each generation of man.

As he viewed humanity from a psychological standpoint he realized that little more motivates our life but the desire for pleasure, power, and self-importance. There is so little free will, so little fully conscious purpose in our actions. He understood this, yet his hands were tied, for he had his family to consider. Living his present life would be a farce, a meaningless repetition, but what else could he do? He had responsibilities to his wife and children. He couldn't go on, and yet he had to go on. He was unable to extricate himself from the course his life was now pursuing, yet even if he could, what would he do? Nothing he imagined had real meaning or value. Every alternative was simply another game, another delusion to distract him from a hopeless reality. His accomplishments and goals now seemed a superfluous triviality. He did not wish to live without meaning or purpose. He could not resign himself to the vulgarity of life, but everywhere was only a void, a nothingness that drained him of will and energy. He had to remain. He was forced to remain, for there was nowhere else to go, and yet he had to go or else die a slow, malingering death.

With this paralyzing dilemma his subconscious set to work in ingenious ways, casting up transient dreams and goals which his groping mind was eager to accept. With such self-delusions he regained his ambition and desire, his sense of importance and self-esteem, but eventually they proved useless, for slowly the truth would dawn as he witnessed the games the world would play. He was haunted everywhere by the absurdity which mocked his existence, and everywhere were the grave reminders that life, as he had known it, was no longer real. Living had become a struggle between boredom and ennui. The world had become a dull, gray emptiness which drained him of the strength to resist. He had no idea where he was going or what he would do. All he knew was that he was tired and depressed, that there was no way out and nowhere to go.

Sitting calmly upon the balcony porch, gazing vacantly into the dark loneliness of night, he only now realized how long it had been since the sun had set. The world had become tranquil and silent as it rested from another day's cycle of futility. The vacuum of space seemed to have descended upon the world, enveloping it in a cold, dark stillness which lulled all things to sleep. Then suddenly into the serenity, a momentary flash streaked across the night sky and faded silently in the west. But just as the falling star fades into nothingness, he too fell just as quickly into the void of despair. The overwhelming hopelessness was just now beginning to converge when suddenly another white star slipped silently from the heavens. With his curiosity aroused, he gazed up into space just in time to witness one more star drop from a formation in the west. He watched with fascination as star after star streaked out from the unknown constellation, blazing a brilliant white light over the utter darkness of a world asleep. Each momentary flash signaled hope in a dying world, only to vanish suddenly and silently from sight. Gazing up into the constellation he wondered what was happening in this remote area of space. What phenomenon could be responsible for such an event?

* * * * *

"You must go on!" he shouted through the storm. And now it was his own turn to be left behind.

Exposed to the alien coldness, the expedition had been reduced to only a few dying members. One by one they had dropped from formation—a crumpled, black mass lying dead and discarded upon the crystalline snow. It had been their fate, and destiny now summoned the end of our own existence.

"But you're the Field Marshal!" I protested. "You're the leader. We can't just leave you."

"No!" he countered. "I am not the Field Marshal. You are the Field Marshal. Now you must lead yourself."

"We'll die anyway," I objected. "What difference does it make?"

"You have a responsibility," he reminded me. "The scouts," and here his voice quivered. "They must be warned before it's too late."

We left him there, as was his wish, and pressed on into the freezing blizzard. More than likely the scouts were already dead, for what else could explain our misfortune? Nothing but their death could account for the failure of our mission, for they were the forerunners, the beacons and guides of our journey.

Flanked on both sides by the black, arrow formation I maneuvered the point against the full force of the storm. Slowly we penetrated the veritable wall of wind. But slowly, one by one, the formation fell to pieces against the unrelenting stress. And yet, those surviving pressed farther into the blizzard, oblivious to their own suffering, inured and numb to the cold.

Eventually, after what seemed many hours, I glanced back through the snow only to realize that I was now alone. The last dying member had long since dropped from sight, leaving me alone to battle the onslaught of the storm. I alone could fulfill the final stage of our mission, and I alone could warn the scouts in time, for there was no one else but me. With a renewed sense of strength and purpose I struggled my way through the wind and snow. Of the once vast expeditionary force I was the sole survivor: a small, black dot moving slowly over a field of white. In all probability I was the last member of a dying, alien race—a race of beings created solely for this mission. Whether we succeeded or failed would be a matter of my own discretion and stamina to resist. And no matter how much pain, no matter how much weariness and exhaustion I would never give in. I would fight to the end! But slowly the bitter, cold pain transformed into a dull numbness over my body. And as time passed, as I struggled farther through the unknown world, an ever-growing weakness began to inhibit my movements. It was no longer pain that hindered my efforts, for pain had long since vanished in overall numbness, nor was it a lack of will to resist, but simply a basic and effective loss of energy.

Eventually the ever-increasing drain brought me to a standstill against the storm. With my little remaining strength it was all I could do to hold myself motionless against the wind. I tried to move forward. My mind ordered my feet to move, but they would not respond. They remained motionless despite my efforts, for with a paralyzing numbness they had long since gone to sleep.

Slowly all sensations withdrew, and the moment I lost control the storm flung me over upon my back. It seemed as though I never even fell, for my insensitive body failed to register the slightest impact in the soft, embracing snow. All I knew was that I was gazing into the dark fury of the storm which now swept past above me. Somewhere, I thought to myself, somewhere above this alien planet was the blackness of space, and in that blackness far above this hostile environment was a world we called our home. It was a home to which we would never return.

Drowsiness soon overcame me. My eyes were weary to close, but I fought it with all my strength and will. Gazing open-eyed into the stormy sky, a mindless daze, an unfeeling consciousness descended upon my soul. I knew that I was dying, that in a few moments I would lose consciousness, and yet all I could do was gaze on into the storm.

* * * * *

He lay motionless upon the lounge chair, gazing up into the oppressive blackness of space. From the balcony porch he had both a bird's-eye view of the world of man and the universe circling above his head. With the serenity of night his mind wandered through the past, pondering over the strangeness of all that had happened. He wondered how he had gotten so far in life, for it was so long ago since that fateful Sunday when he had realized the truth. It was so long ago since he had lost his illusions and become conscious of life. Time seemed to have stopped, and the interim was simply a vacuum without progression. He seemed suspended in a lingering, trans-dimensional awareness, a lost limbo of timelessness.

Of course it took some time to reach this state. At first it simply began as a growing dissatisfaction. His goals and accomplishments seemed to have lost all meaning. Nothing he did really seemed to matter, and so it was with difficulty that he managed to struggle, day by day, through the painful routine of life. It was for his family, he reminded himself. It was for his family that he was forcing himself to accomplish what had to be done, but could it be any different? Another life, another time, would anything every really change?

Eventually time passed. The children soon grew

into adults. Like fading dreams they vanished into the past with lives and families of their own. And his wife, his so dearly beloved, how she had changed with the mere passage of time. Once so enchanting, she had quickly lost her youth and beauty, becoming a plain, empty, worn-out shell. And not just physically. It was hard to believe that such changes could occur, but with the loss of physical attraction her personality and spirit had also lost their charm. No longer the focus of attention, with children and admirers long since gone, so vanished all her sense of importance. Having nothing more to do in life she became bitter and cynical toward the world around her. She complained about everything, nagged about the smallest trifles, implying that it was his fault things weren't different. It seemed impossible that his dream could have decayed into such a nettling, old thing. He was amazed that his love, the one thing he believed to be true and eternal, could have dissolved before him into open disgust. What was once a burning flame in his heart had now been reduced to an annoying embarrassment. It was as if life had somehow played a trick on him, as though he had been a lifelong player in some cheap and stupid game.

Of course it was as much his fault as it was hers, for he himself was nothing much to admire. Since retirement he had become a weary, old man with nothing to do. Without drive or ambition, without direction or purpose, he simply moped about like a living corpse. In a sense she was justified in blaming him for their boredom, but what else was there to do? It wasn't really his fault, for life itself seemed to be in error. Every action was simply another meaningless repetition. Every goal was simply another childish game without significance. He became acutely aware of the absurdity of life, of the senselessness of mindless, predetermined activity. But there was nothing more to do, nothing but to sit back and watch the next round of life repeat the same useless struggles.

He sank back in the lounge chair, totally engulfed by the calmness of night, totally entombed by his own void of indifference. With closed eyes he was unaware of what now transpired above his head. In his disillusionment and empty dreams nothing he did made the slightest impact, but far away in another world strange forces were just now taking shape. They were forces that would transform his destiny.

He had closed his eyes while reminiscing, and on opening them he was astonished by a vision from the north. The sky was on fire! Streamers, rays, fountains of light, rainbows and curtains of glowing motion. It was a projection of color folding and shimmering in space, an infusion of lights warping in the darkness. They were crystalline lights, shimmering and hissing in the void, sparkling like a cavern of diamonds and gems. The northern lights played upon his soul, laughing and dancing, smiling and soothing. They radiated a warmth and comfort that mesmerized his soul.

They were like the fireworks of childhood, the fireworks he had saved all his allowance to purchase. Fountains, sparklers, skyrockets—an arsenal of projected colors illuminating the night. And yet it was over too soon. The display faded in an explosive shower of sparkling light, leaving only the bleakness of a costly disappointment. It was real, but it didn't last. It existed only for the moment, and then it was gone.

And just the same was the disappointment in these new celestial fireworks. Unfolding its treasures within the emptiness of space, suspended in the blackness of night, the crystalline lights shone like a beacon, a doorway to another world, an enchanted realm of meaning and life. But suddenly, without warning, the fluctuating luminesence faded into darkness. The ghostly apparitions slowly disappeared. Within moments not a trace was left. Darkness returned as the aurora vanished from sight—a dream, a memory, no longer a reality.

* * * * *

I sat motionless in my seat, staring vacantly at the darkness of the screen. The auditorium was deserted. Not a soul was in sight. Each screen was an empty mirror devoid of movement, reflecting only the shadows of an abandoned world. The sudden revelation brought about passive quiescence. Completely absorbed in the silence and stillness I remained a calm spectator within the void. It was, of course, only a show, a real play enacted for my sole benefit. Staged and produced by my own delusions it naturally cast me in the leading role, yet I had no idea how long I had played the part.

After the initial shock of understanding, the oppressive atmosphere engulfed me in a motionless vacuum. The stillness of the theater made me feel lonely and isolated as I scanned row after row of empty seats. Over to the side, massive supports extended so far into the darkness that I failed to see any form of ceiling. On gazing up I became dwarfed by a feeling of insignificance. I was alone—a pinpoint existence surrounded by emptiness. The theater intended for thousands was now entertaining only one guest, its grandeur existing solely for my miniscule appreciation.

Suddenly, a woman's faint cry for help roused me from my trance. I stumbled through the half-darkness and entered the lobby. I was stunned by the silence of what was once a busy tourist center. Not only did the Structure seem deserted, but the power was blacked-out. The only light filtered in through an occasional window from the overcast sky. What's more, all heating units seemed to have frozen over. A cold draft passed intermittently through the corridors like some alien intruder in search of prey.

I was traveling toward the faint cry when approaching footsteps rang out down the gloomy corridor. A vaguely discernible figure was coming into view. My heart leapt at the sight of Katon's approach, but it sank just as quickly on noticing his aloofness.

"What's wrong?" I asked. "What's happening to the Structure?"

He stood silent for a few moments, gazing off into the darkness. He seemed lost in a trance, his eyes focusing on some distant world, a world beyond the limits of my extension. His voice seemed alien, remotely detached as though uttered with godlike wisdom and finality.

"It is," he replied, and his voice seemed to echo through the darkness of the empty passage, "the beginning of the endless dream . . ."

In the distance, the voice of a dying woman conveyed a message, but I was too far away to understand her words, too far away to help even if I could. For I myself was approaching an infinite end. Katon urged me forward but was also dismayed by the trial which he knew would soon be mine. We entered the room and found the strangely familiar woman lying helpless upon the bed. Her eyes gazed up through weakness and exhaustion. She tried to speak, but only faint whispers escaped her fatigue. Struck while in the performance of her duty, sacrificed for the cause, the price for our questionable victory would soon be her life.

Katon lifted the small, fragile creature and carried her out into the cold, dark afternoon. As he laid her gently upon the soft, white snow her face gradually grew more familiar and intimate. She seemed to resemble someone from the past, perhaps from a dream or from a former life. It was then that I saw the blue, crystal ring which sparkled and glowed. Her eyes gazed lifelessly into the overcast sky from which flakes of snow fell gently to the ground. Perhaps she could still see the formations of birds escaping south for the winter. Perhaps that is what Katon wished her to see.

Her voice echoed through my mind—something important she was trying to say, but something I could never hear. The soft emphasis of her words slowly weakened. The words melted, then faded like the snowflakes that touched my hands. The silence grew. The serene stillness emerged, creating an impossible world of white snow, a gray overcast sky, and flocks of birds like arrows drifting south.

Chapter Six:
THE END OF LIFE

Falling stars for lightning skies and battlefields of cosmic fights.

Falling stars for future dreams with wonderlands and child delights.

Falling stars for other worlds where secret loves and dreams come true.

Falling stars from endless dreams—the zero point is you.

I HAD TRAVELED for many days through the deserted Structure, spending many cold nights scrambling to survive. I had no idea what caused the disaster, and so I wandered about exploring all possibilities, searching everywhere for some clue to the enigma. Throughout the empty corridors time seemed to have become eternal. The Structure was simply a lifeless shell of the past—the deserted ruins of what used to be. Yet nowhere were there signs of bodies or debris. Nowhere was there evidence of struggle or disorder. Everyone simply vanished in the night, leaving no trace of their sudden departure. All that was left was the lingering silence of isolation, the perfect stillness of an abandoned world.

Katon had once again mysteriously disappeared. This time I was forced to conclude I had been consciously abandoned. Perhaps, after all, it was for my own good. For the strongest trees stand apart from all others.

After many days of fruitless search I found myself wandering aimlessly through vacant passages, wondering whether anything mattered. Was this the end of life? Had it all become hopeless? I sat dejectedly and pondered my fate. With the world destroyed was there any reason to go on? Was there any value to further action? What would it accomplish? What difference would it make with no one around?

Lost in thought, absorbed in silence, I was jarred by peals of laughter coming from below. I peered into the depths and could only now discern a dim glow filtering up the dark stairway. I scrambled step by step down to the source of life. Moment by moment the giggling and laughter grew louder as each step brought me closer to the ever-growing light. I was overwhelmed in anticipation of this new development. Could the survivors offer an explanation for the crisis? Would they know what was happening and what should now be done? With such thoughts I descended through the darkness until I emerged into a fully-lit, Sub-Basement room.

Apparently my appearance was as much a shock to the survivors as it was to me, for the children, who were formerly screeching with laughter, suddenly ceased their antics and gazed up in astonishment. Dropping in out of nowhere I had apparently invaded the private setting of a domestic, family bedroom. But the second shock was even greater than the first, for I suddenly chanced upon something odd crouching off in the corner. The Madman and I exchanged looks of disbelief.

You can't be real," he maintained calmly, and yet he trembled spasmodically. "You're supposed to be dead."

"I'm not dead. Maybe you're the one who's dead." And I walked over to find out.

"Get away from me!" he yelled, jumping up from the floor. "When I awoke you weren't anywhere around. You said you would watch over me, and yet you had vanished in the night. You weren't there then, and you're not here now."

"Of course he's here," said the lady seated on the bed. Absorbed in her knitting she had noted my entrance with indifference. "Now don't be rude," she scolded, "and stop insulting our guest. He doesn't look dead to me. Be a good dear and apologize." It was strange to see such erratic behavior respond to such mild authority, but slowly and hesitantly the Madman obeyed.

"But you said you would stay with me," he whined.

I explained what had happened: how the blackout had left me surrounded by demons; how on calling out into the darkness no one answered; how I became hysterical realizing he had vanished. My account had apparently pacified his fears, for with his mind at ease he sank back to the floor.

"I just wanted to go home," he cried softly.

"You are home," said the woman, "and everything will be all right." And suddenly it dawned on me that this was his family. This was the Madman's wife, and scattered about the bedroom were their children. It was hard to determine the exact number, for they kept moving about and hiding underneath the bed and blankets. Slowly the noise and laughter resumed as the children began chasing each other playfully about. I became disoriented by the movement and the sudden turn of events.

"What's happening?" I asked helplessly.

"What's happening?" he remarked, offhandedly. "Why nothing's happening. Nothing at all."

"But haven't you noticed the absence?" I asked, gesturing above. "The Structure is deserted!"

"I don't know about the Structure," he answered. "And I don't care. All I know is what happens down here, and everything's the same as it's always been."

I realized that questioning the Madman was useless, and so I sank down beside him and began surveying the room.

"What's this?" I asked, for only now did I notice thousands of books crowding the walls from floor to ceiling. Overflowing shelves were jammed with books, all of which were in chaotic disorder, seemingly piled together and stuffed wherever space allowed. And where space did not allow, the floor provided ample room for the overspill of books. Multitudes lay scattered haphazardly along the floor. Many more were piled high in tumbled stacks against the walls. Was this the elusive library?

"It's my bookstore," corrected the Madman with pride. "I've collected many first editions and many rare, out-of-print books. You'll find ancient manuscripts and priceless documents by unknown authors. Secret works by the greatest literary giants are also at your disposal. All the books you've ever dreamed of are now within reach. Anything you can imagine is awaiting your discovery." Snatching an old, tattered folder off the floor, he opened it to crinkly papyrus. "Here, for example, is the original manuscript of an ancient philosopher. It is the greatest treatise ever inscribed on the nature of reality. It has never been published, and in the entire universe this is the only copy—penned by the author himself." With that he tossed the manuscript carelessly into the corner. "Look around," he added exuberantly, "take your time before you purchase. Take all the time in the world." He then sauntered over to join his wife and children.

My heart began throbbing. Could this be it? After a lifelong search could this be the moment, the unraveling of all mysteries, the revelation of my dreams? I was giddy and dizzy all at the same time. After an eternity of ignorance, my goal was unfolding before me eyes. At long last I would know the truth. And nothing could stand in my way. Nothing could bar me from this new eternity.

The room seemed to be closing in, the walls of books pressuring me with their conspicuous presence, each book demanding to be opened and read. And yet I had no idea where to begin. Scrolls, novels, booklets; volumes upon volumes of ancient stories and doctrines; thousands upon thousands of strange, obscure works; a gallery of mysterious writers and philosophers all waiting anxiously for the revelation to begin. My heart fluttered with anticipation. Here I was amidst a treasure-trove of knowledge. Here I was before a whole new vista of life, and I knew I would never again be the same. Shuffling through a dusty pile of books I pulled out the thinnest, most quickly assimilable pamphlet and eagerly nestled down into the posh comforter to read. It was a small, blue booklet covered with childish drawings and quotations.

STICKMAN'S ATTEMPT AT SELF-REALIZATION

OR

THE TRAGIC FATE OF A NONENTITY

BY THE MADMAN

REVOLUTIONARY PRESS UNLIMITED

A SUBSIDIARY OF DREAMS, INCORPORATED

STICKMAN WALKED DOWN THE STREET.
EVERYTHING WAS NICE AND PEACEFUL. "IT'S
ALL SO SIMPLE," HE EXCLAIMED TO HIMSELF.
AND SO IT WAS. PEOPLE TALKED. BIRDS SANG.
"THE WORLD IS SO STRANGE," HE THOUGHT TO
HIMSELF. FOR EVERYTHING WAS MADE OUT OF
LINES!

LOOKING OVER HIS NEW SURROUNDINGS,
STICKMAN WAS READY FOR ACTION. "WHAT SHOULD
I DO?" HE ASKED HIMSELF. AND SO HE LOOKED
HERE AND THERE TO FIND AN ANSWER, BUT NOWHERE
COULD HE FIND A PURPOSE FOR HIS LIFE. HE
LOOKED UNDER ROCKS. HE GAZED INTO HOUSES.
HE CLIMBED UP TREES AND SCANNED NEW HORIZONS,
BUT NOWHERE COULD HE FIND ANYTHING TO DO.

"I DON'T UNDERSTAND," SAID STICKMAN TO
HIMSELF. FOR HE KNEW DEEP INSIDE THERE MUST
BE SOME REASON FOR HIS LIFE. THERE MUST BE
SOME REASON FOR THE EXISTENCE OF THE WORLD.
IT WAS ONLY A MATTER OF FINDING OUT "WHY?"
AND SO STICKMAN WANDERED ABOUT, ASKING
EVERYONE HE MET THE MEANING AND PURPOSE OF
LIFE.

"THE MEANING OF LIFE," SAID ONE MAN,
"IS TO LIVE!" "TO MAKE MONEY!" SAID
ANOTHER. "TO RAISE A FAMILY AND BE SUCCESS-
FUL." "TO BE HAPPY AND ENJOY YOURSELF."
"TO HELP ONE ANOTHER." "TO LOVE ONE
ANOTHER." "TO LOVE GOD." "TO WORSHIP GOD."
"TO BE GOOD." "TO DO GOOD." "TO BE THIS."
"TO BE THAT." "TO DO THIS." "TO DO THAT."
AND SO ON, AND SO FORTH WENT THE PITIFUL
EXCUSES, EACH OF WHICH WAS TRYING TO OUTDO
AND OUT-JUSTIFY THE OTHER. BUT AS STICKMAN
GAZED DOWN INTO THE BUSY STREET EVERY REASON
AND EVERY ACTION SEEMED EQUALLY ABSURD. WITH
PEOPLE BUSTLING ABOUT LIKE TINY ANTS, EVEN
THE MOST SERIOUS RESPONSE SEEMED JUST
ANOTHER SILLY GAME.

"BUT THIS CAN'T BE!" SAID STICKMAN TO
HIMSELF. "THERE MUST BE MORE TO LIFE THAN
JUST PLAYING AROUND!" AND SO STICKMAN SET
OUT TO FIND THE ANSWER TO LIFE. NO MATTER
WHAT THE COST STICKMAN WAS INTENT ON
DISCOVERING THE TRUTH. AND HIS INTENTIONS
WOULD SUCCEED, FOR IT WOULD BE HIS MIS-
FORTUNE TO COME TO TERMS WITH THE PROFESSOR,
THE ONE PERSON IN THE WORLD WHO COULD BRING
HIM FACE-TO-FACE WITH REALITY. IT WAS A
NIGHTMARE REALITY THAT WOULD DRIVE HIM
INSANE.

TO BE CONTINUED

Curious and excited I rummaged through the books for a similar-sized pamphlet, yet I failed to uncover the continuing story. In dismay I requested the Madman's help.

"Oh, that," he said with amusement. "It's somewhere around." Then suddenly his face became grave and thoughtful. "Are you sure you're ready for it?"

I stifled a laugh, for obviously the pamphlet was of a juvenile nature, almost to the point of comic-book simplicity.

"At any rate the copy you found is now yours. The charge will come with the concluding sequel." With that he laughed haughtily and returned to his seat. I was bewildered by the Madman's transformation, for since mentioning the bookstore he had become a rational, coherent, fast-talking salesman. He dealt with me with businesslike efficiency as though I were somehow inferior to him. I dismissed it as all a part of his madness and proceeded with a systematic search of the room.

I scanned the shelves for the Stickman pamphlet and was aroused by many compelling titles: *Evolutionary Consciousness*; *Warriors of Life*; *Zen Foot-Notes*; *Movies and the Meaning of Life*; and *The Endless Dream*. I felt like devouring them all at once, yet held myself back to finishing one at a time, if only I could find one to finish, if only I could find one at all. How to Write a Book seemed interesting, but as I glanced through the work I found only mathematical formulas and proofs. My Book seemed even more exciting, but as I opened it I was both surprised and disappointed. It was a bound manuscript of blank pages. The author had not even started, and yet it was already in print. *Structural Revolutions* was apparently a theoretical history of a movement. Another bizarre fairy tale was *The Adventures of Duckling*.

As I continued my search I recalled the rumors of underground libraries carrying unauthorized books. Slowly I began wondering about The Time Has Come, the dream-book that had literally initiated my journey. Was it possible that somewhere beneath the dusty piles of books my most longed-for treasure awaited my discovery? I realized that of all places this library would surely have the book. With mounting excitement I once again requested the Madman's help.

"The Time Has Come?" he repeated in a puzzled tone, and my hopes fell with such tenuous uncertainty. "Oh yes," he replied after a moment's thought, and my heart once again leapt for joy. "You mean Katon's work. But that's no book. That's an unfinished journal. He never did complete it before his death."

"What are you saying?" I exclaimed. "Katon's not dead! I spoke to him only a few days ago."

"Are you certain?" asked the Madman doubtfully. "Many people are mistaken for him. And many people see him only in their minds. Fanciful thinking. It's as simple as that."

"But I tell you it was him!" I protested. "He told me so himself. And as for the incomplete journal, it's a complete book. In fact for awhile I had a bound copy myself. I lost it though, but I did kill for it."

The Madman only smiled in a condescending manner.

"The way I read it, Katon burned the last segment of his journal before disappearing beyond the West Walls—presumed dead at the age of twenty. Thus the journal, by its autobiographical nature, necessarily remains incomplete."

"Twenty!" I exclaimed, agreeing with the Madman's reasoning and yet surprised over Katon's age.

"Why?" asked the Madman. "How old did you think he was?"

"I'm not certain," I replied. "Whenever we met it was always dark and gloomy. I never did get a clear look at his face. However, now that you mention it, he did seem young. But then on the other hand he seemed to be old, eternally old. I don't understand it."

"Well, at any rate," said the Madman, "I was his closest contact so I should know." And here his words became dreamy as he began to reminisce. "It was at the Symposium of Revolutionists that I first laid eyes upon our leader. The conference was held at my teacher's mountain retreat beyond the West Walls. Leaders were invited from all around. Representatives of Dreams, Incorporated and Subliminal Projections were present; so too were Iris, the Professor, and the Professor's Assistant. Nearly all the authors in this library attended the occasion. Also making an appearance were accomplished artists, poets, mathematicians, and musicians. Spiritual, intellectual, and artistic leaders of all types filled the house from top to bottom. The rooms buzzed with conversation, each creative genius exchanging ideas on his latest venture. The rooms were a swirl of energy in motion, the bursting energy of creative expression. Scattered groups surrounding various paintings and sculptures were engaged in debates over their interpretation and meaning. Literary groups off to the side were excitedly discussing their latest novels and plays. Secluded from the noisy crowds in out-of-the-way niches, poets were reciting their newest lines. Philosophers and scientists discoursed over their insights and theories. Mystics related their revelations and dreams. And above all the clamor, musicians and composers studied each other's works, playing occasionally on pianos, violins, and flutes. The rooms surged with creative life and power flowing about in ecstatic release. But beyond all this, upon the balcony porch a dark silhouette stood motionless against the night. All alone, outside the life and light, Katon stood gazing into the coldness of space."

Evidently it was time to sleep, for the children began spreading pillows and mattresses upon the floor. Eventually the bed, which was only a pile of mattresses, had been thoroughly dismantled. The scattered remains were piled high with blankets, forming one giant bed nearly spanning the entire library. I rose to my feet and was about to leave when the Madman insisted I stay for the night.

"You're not through yet, are you?" Obviously I had only begun to assimilate the library, and so he cajoled. "Stay here tonight. That way you can start fresh, first thing in the morning." His wife nodded her consent, and so did I.

Despite the awkwardness of the situation I had nowhere else to go, and so I accepted the hospitality of the Madman. Climbing under the covers soon ended all feelings of embarrassment, for the children began frolicking about, jumping all around me in excitement over their new-found playmate. I was given no rest until the light was put out and their mother told them to settle down and sleep.

The following days found me completely absorbed in literature. Night after night I was the reluctant guest who was eagerly persuaded to stay another night. As the days passed I became so familiar to the household that I actually felt I was part of the family. The children literally shared in the feeling of closeness, for they followed me all around, adopting me into their fantasies and games. It was as though I had finally found my refuge, a brief respite from the madness of life, ironically within a Madman's home. I seemed to have lost myself in another world, the dream world of a returning childhood. I had no idea why I felt so close to the family. And yet it seemed as though I belonged there, as though I had always been there, however far away.

I spent many days perusing the library, concentrating for many hours without rest, bewitched and obsessed with the Madman's books. I never did find The Time Has Come nor Stickman's concluding sequel, however I did read many stories of life in strange and secretive worlds. Dreams, Incorporated was about a dream which became real. It was about a point of consciousness trapped within a spherical void. Nothing enters. Nothing emerges. The consciousness dreams. The void becomes light. Crystalline colors flow and merge. But the consciousness awakens. Darkness and void. The light existed only in the mind, only in the point, the interface which does not tangibly exist. An illusion . . . then dream. Crystal lights, movement, gentle warmth—but within darkness! Hallucinations. Madness without repercussions. The rainbow colors continue. Within a void, reality and dream are one. The prismatic display expands, reflected and refracted within the void, a play of forces, waves of pure unimaginable light, dancing, swirling, laughing in subtle shades of color, a cosmic symphony orchestrated by dreams and thought.

Structural Revolutions was another strange fantasy. It was the historical account of the dissipation of the Structure. What was interesting was the absence of a date or point of reference, as though the Structural collapse had taken place all along. A random fragment seemed pertinent to my situation.

Chapter 0.999...
Confrontation in Subliminal Projections

The movement was incredible. The ray extended infinitely in all directions. Without prescience or warning the Revolutionary forces emerged from nowhere. Their movements were amazing in their subtlety. The disparate elements gradually encompassed and overwhelmed the Structure. Once the formation was realized it was already too late. The fragmentation had solidified into a whole. With only a momentary pause the Revolutionists triangulated and attacked. The offensive took the form of a circular ray. It came from everywhere. The battle was over before it had begun. With minimal resistance the Revolutionists penetrated the

118

Structure, violated its premises, releasing a chaotic turbulence in their wake.

The Madman himself recounted adventures and intrigue at the mountain retreat. He told of the field trips with his teacher in search of some biological specimen, some chrysalis or butterfly on the verge of extinction. He recalled the story behind the Symposium of Revolutionists: the conclusions that were reached along with the goals that were set. Reflecting over his experiments with the Professor, the Madman revealed their investigations and breakthroughs. Katon was also a frequenter of the mountain retreat. The Madman described their many encounters: how they would spend days discussing plans and strategies, formulating new theories and analyzing the old, but most of all how they grew to become close friends. He explained how Katon had given him his unfinished journal, The Time Has Come, and how he himself had been present the night Katon passed beyond the West Walls.

After what seemed simply another fascinating day of study I settled down for the night and had the strangest dream. I was somewhere in the wilderness far beyond the West Walls. The Professor and I were watching a shiny, black caterpillar spinning itself an intricate cocoon. I was entranced by the spectacle of such a small creature working with such meticulous care. Each strand of silk was placed methodically in a design worthy of the most skilled craftsman.

"The caterpillar," said the Professor, "being a truly noble creature spins its own living tomb from which it emerges either a totally different and magnificent creature, or emerges not at all."

Around me I found several other caterpillars busily engaged in the same activity, equally absorbed in building their retreat with consummate skill and determination. But on glancing up I was shocked to find a bird plucking a caterpillar from its half-open cocoon. The winged monster poised high in the bush with the squirming morsel between its beak, and with a quick gulp the potential butterfly was removed forever from the world. I could scarcely believe what had just taken place. My spirit was repulsed by such a fate. How could such depravity exist? What was responsible for such savagery and horror?

"It happens all the time," said the Professor as though reading my mind. "On every blade of grass, beneath every rock, behind every leaf and twig the endless battle rages on. There is no mercy in the cosmic scheme. Pain and destruction, misery and torment, a vicious cycle of predator and prey, a nightmare world of violence and murder are all an integral part of the Structure—a Structure that has existed throughout eternity. It is an eternity filled with horrible death and horrible life, a perverted universe of madness and chaos. Yet there is no other."

We stood awhile in silence. My mind was rendered impotent by the revelation. I was unable to comprehend the existence of such a world. And slowly my thoughts drifted back to the balcony porch, to the Madman's teacher who sheltered each generation of butterflies. During the fall she collected hundreds of cocoons, storing them in jars on the balcony porch. When spring came the butterflies emerged and flew away. She was their unknown guardian, protecting them from a bloodthirsty world.

"Does it matter?" said a man's voice.

My heart pounded from the sudden transition. "Does what matter?" I asked the Professor of my dream.

There was silence, void, and a vacant stare.

"Does what matter?" I asked again.

"The vanity extends as far as the eye can see. It extends as far as the memory recalls and the mind comprehends."

Surprisingly I ignored his enigmatic answer, for something more important came to mind. Slowly and carefully I put forth a metaphysical koan.

"What is a summer," I asked, my heart throbbing in anticipation, "with one less butterfly?"

All things seemed to stop and listen. The world grew calm as it awaited the final answer. A soft, yet resonant voice came from everywhere—the mountains, the trees, the sky.

"Nothing . . ." said the voice from above, fading away—merging with the silence.

Chapter Seven:
ASYLUM

---

*Madness is a precondition to life. Its form
simply varies among different animals.*

—THE MADMAN

THROUGH THE DARKNESS I felt I was being watched, the presence of consciousness bearing down upon my soul. Through my dreams I struggled back and opened my eyes.

"Hooray!" shouted the children with shrieks and giggles. Apparently they had been standing vigil over my body, silently awaiting my eventual return. Obviously I had overslept, and for fear of waking me they were forbidden to play. Now that I was conscious they screeched for joy, running about in ecstatic release.

"What time is it?" I groaned, my mind beclouded and my vision blurred.

"It's late," said a voice from the past. "It's almost too late."

A vaguely familiar figure came into view. The hazy image gradually cleared as my blinking eyes focused on the surprising, yet welcome sight of the Professor's Assistant.

"I see you've found the library," he remarked with a sly, cheerful grin.

"It took all my life, but here I am. What are you doing here?" I asked, overjoyed at the knowledge that he too had somehow survived. "I thought you were dead."

"On the contrary!" he exclaimed. "We all thought you were dead. We've been looking all over, but you were nowhere around."

"Well, here I am. Why didn't you wake me?"

"I never disturb anyone who's asleep," he explained, "for they must awaken on their own. You know," he added in criticism, "it's rude to keep people waiting. The children have been expecting you for hours."

"Well here I am," I announced for the third time (I had become obsessed with counting numbers). "Now what can I do for you?" I asked politely as though I were the Madman's bookseller. His face grew crestfallen and dismayed.

"Don't you know what's happening? The Structure is dissolving. It may very well be the beginning of the end."

"Everything's deserted. That's all I know. I don't know how or why, but no one's around. They've all disappeared."

"For one thing," he explained, "they're not gone. They're simply hiding. They're scared, for they know that the time has come. It is the final Revolutionary war. The outcome of this long-dreaded, yet inevitable battle will determine our course for all eternity. For even the slightest deviation at the start will magnify toward the end. The time has come for the Revolutionists to free themselves of the Structure and become unbounded. This Structure is simply the facade binding the manifestations of the world. Instead we must confront the source itself. This force, which has been mushrooming since the world began, has come to a head and must be overcome. There is no other choice, for in order to alter our course, in order to escape the confines of the Structure, we must challenge the force binding us in this form. We must converge and project ourselves beyond the West Walls. We must extend our limits into the unknown. It is the only way for man to be free, to rid himself of the illusions which rationalize his insanity. It is the only way for man to be real, to overcome the Structural bondage of life. There will be no second chance," he warned, "for it is now or never."

"But what should we do?" I asked helplessly. "What can we do? We're only two people."

"Three people," chirped the Madman, hidden beneath the blankets.

"I'm not sure," the Professor's Assistant replied honestly. "We're powerless for the moment. But that's why I'm here. We must rendezvous with the other rebels. All our efforts must be focused upon penetrating the West Walls. for only there, only outside the Structure will our actions have any effect. Only there can we reshape our destiny. The key lies in our ability to withstand the impact of the void. The future of mankind, the destiny of the human race depends upon our eventual success. It is up to us, and we must succeed. For only through our victory can man be free. Others have tried. Most have either been destroyed or driven insane in conflicts beyond the West Walls. But the Structural collapse has revealed a pathway circumventing the area of conflict—a secret passage into the most distant regions of the west. It is the last chance for those who dare penetrate the truth. For one split second the curtains will rise on the scheme of life. For one brief instant the universe will be vulnerable to meta-morphosis. At last, man can glimpse the subliminal reality. But our only hope is to venture beyond the Structure, beyond the West Walls to the end of our journey. For only there will the vision unfold, only there can we find our new eternity. And that is why I have come, for the passage begins here, somewhere close by in the mysterious realm of the Sub-Base-ment."

"No!" cried a voice quivering under the blan-kets. "You don't know what you're saying. You don't know what you're doing. It'll be the end! You'll all be killed! You'll all die a horrible, agonizing death!"

"Is that the Madman?" asked the Professor's As-sistant. I nodded in embarrassment. "Well that ex-plains it. You see, rumors are that only a few rebels have actually found the secret passage. And of those who have, the Madman is the only one who has yet returned. The Madman is the only one who can show us the way."

"I won't!" screamed the muffled voice. "You can't make me! I'll never go back! Do you hear me? Nev-er!" Then suddenly his voice grew calm and com-posed. "It's not what you think. You see, I've been there. I know what it's like. I was lucky to escape with even half my sanity. And if you think I'm crazy now, you should see me when I'm truly mad. Others are trapped there just as you will be trapped. Yes," he explained gravely, "even Katon himself can never return."

"But don't you see?" asked the Professor's Assis-tant. "It's our only chance. Nothing else matters any longer. We must find out once and for all before it's too late."

"It's already too late!" screamed the Madman, re-lapsing into his normally distraught self. "You'll destroy everything!"

"Everything is already destroyed. We have no choice."

"It's madness!" screeched the Madman, his voice trembling with fear. "You're fools. You don't know what you're up against. It's the void! It's unfettered reality! Quintessential and unlimited! Infinitely extended! Omnipotently present! You have no chance!"

Realizing that he would get nowhere with the Madman, the Professor's Assistant rose and motioned for me to follow.

"It's getting late," he remarked while moving toward the door to the Sub-Basement. "And we must be there on time—at precisely the right place and precisely the right moment. We'll simply have to find it without him. Are you coming?" he asked the Madman for the last time.

"No!" screamed the voice from under the blankets, his body trembling in fits of hysterics. "You'll destroy everything! You'll unleash a nightmare into the world!" And then suddenly he broke into moronic gibberish. "Life is nice!" he chanted over and over. "Life is nice! Life is nice! I have no qualms! Life is nice!"

We left him there mumbling like an idiot, his entire face and body hidden beneath the covers. What I remembered most was the family's sadness over my departure. The mother and children, the family I had come to know so well, were heartbroken over my departure. It was as though they somehow knew I would never return, as though fate itself were now parting us forever. Yet all relationships must eventually end, and if it wasn't now then it would simply be later. The dream was good while it lasted, but urged on to newer realms I closed the cellar door on the sad countenance of childhood memories.

A sudden coldness greeted our entry into the Sub-Basement. The contrast between the warm, cozy library and this nether world of shadowy isolation was astounding. The uncanniness made me half wish I were back in bed, but with the Professor's Assistant goading me forward I mustered my courage and proceeded forth into the unknown.

"I'm not sure of its location," he whispered in confidence. "But it's somewhere close by."

As we continued through the dark passage the memory of my nightmare returned. Previous narrow escapes made me aware that I was pressing my luck, that sooner or later I would eventually succumb. An eeriness in the air kept me glancing about in anticipation. At any moment I was ready to break into panic and run. I shuddered at the feeling that we were being watched, that demonic forces were observing our passage through a world where we didn't belong. The foreboding seemed now to be more pronounced than ever, as though the Structural collapse had somehow unleashed the subhuman denizens of this realm. Now with complete freedom they seemed to be lurking everywhere, in the shadows, around corners, ready at any moment to take their revenge. I was anticipating our doom when the sudden sounds of pursuit sent us scrambling for cover. Peering out from under cover we watched an abomination running wildly through the corridor. He was blubbering, cursing, and chanting as he went. But as he drew near we were surprised by the distorted features of the Madman. His distraught face was twisted by fear and insanity, his body seemingly at odds with the environment, as though he were suffering simply by his presence in this world.

"There you are!" he cried out. "I thought you were lost."

"You've changed your mind?" asked the Professor's Assistant.

"No!" cringed the Madman, suddenly draining of color. "I have no qualms. For life is nice. I'll simply show you the way. You'll never find it without me."

The Madman then took the lead, pulling us farther from the warmth and safety of his library. As we traveled through the Sub-Basement we were plagued by the incessant chanting of the Madman. "Life is nice," he would repeat as if to ward off demons. "Life is nice. Life is nice. I have no qualms. For life is nice." The rhythmic chant went on and on and would have been comical had it not apparently worked. Without thought both the Professor's Assistant and I gradually joined in the chant as we followed the Madman through his demented labyrinth. We zigzagged through narrow corridors and were sidetracked into a maze of offbeat paths and doorways. Climbing up and down ladders and ropes we found our way into hidden rooms through small portholes and secret entrances. Eventually, after descending a spiraling staircase, we found ourselves entering an underground world of some sort.

"Here we are!"

It was a stage completely surrounded by darkness. In the center was a table covered with books and pamphlets all of which were either unfinished or disordered. It was our task to finish and rearrange the jigsaw puzzle, interconnecting, rewriting, re-incorporating diverse elements. We set to work immediately.

The form was considered to be necessarily infinite. Thus an expression was required vast enough to encompass its scope. An equation was developed which would convey the magnitude in a logical form. But through its infinite nature the equation itself became a paradox. The variable was an entity whose value was unknown, but which had a definite value nonetheless, a value that was to be discovered by solving the equation. Thus we proceeded:

$$Z = .999...$$

$$10Z = 9.999...$$

$$10Z - Z = 9.999... - .999...$$

$$9Z = 9$$

$$Z = 1$$

$$.999... = 1$$

Thus an infinite extension of an incompletion can result in a unified wholeness.

That seemed to be applicable, but I had no idea exactly how.

A geometric parallel to the algebraic paradox was that of the infinite extension of a ray. Was not an infinite extension itself a contradiction in terms? The paradox aroused heated debate. One faction contended that an infinite distance would require an infinite time to traverse, and consequently the object would never reach its appointed goal. This group subsequently succumbed to apathy and became slow and lethargic in their movement. Whereas another faction reasoned that an infinite speed was all that was necessary. This group consequently sped up their movement, for although an infinite distance must be traversed, an infinite speed would counter the transcendental effect.

However other factions argued that an infinite distance, by definition, can never be traversed, no matter how great the speed (even to infinity), for the transcendent distance will always continue to linger on. What's more, such factions denied the possibility of an infinite speed, maintaining that it was physically impossible within normal space-time.

And yet one strange faction held the premise that space-time was not normal, that on the scale of the universe it was actually warped and that consequently conventional laws no longer applied. This group laughed at the folly of movement, considering it a mere striving after the wind. They argued and proved, at least theoretically, that given sufficient time the ray would eventually warp back upon itself. Hence frantic striving was foolhardy and to no avail.

Another faction contended that once a goal, any goal, was posited then it was no longer infinite (unless infinity was the goal). Thus it was only a matter of time and speed before the point would be reached, but it would be reached. They argued that space and distance were not at issue here, for space is defined only by its geometric confinement. Thus the ray and its theoretically appointed extension necessarily control the nature of the situation. Hence anything can be accomplished if it be only willed and defined.

There was panic. The stage lights flashed out and we were on our own. It was another failure of power. We were alone in the darkness without sense of direction. There was a movement. Was it the Madman? Was it the Professor's Assistant? Echoing footsteps trotted about in nervous agitation.

"Over here!" called out an anonymous voice, as though discovering the focal point. "It was here all the time." Blind and disoriented, my unidentified companion and I followed the voice through the darkness. We reached the location and waited as calmly as we could. It was hard to tell who was who.

"Well?" I asked after a few moments of silence. "Nothing's happening."

"Patience," the voice remarked. And I realized with uneasiness that I could not distinguish between the voices of the Professor's Assistant and the Madman. In fact I could not even recognize my own. In this netherworld I sounded like a different person. Who was I? What was my name? Was it merely "I?"

The voice continued its instructions. "It must be exactly the precise moment—just the right sequence of events in both time and space."

We were finally free within the darkness. There was nothing to do but wait. We stood silently in anticipation for the right moment to occur. And it did occur.

"Over here," said someone. And once again we followed blindly through the darkness. The feeling was of a narrow passage. Once we entered, it would totally restrict our movement, our sense of freedom. But it was a passage which might very well lead us beyond the West Walls. It was a risk we would have to take, a metaphysical gamble and game of chance.

I crossed the threshold and suddenly realized that I was alone. A certain calmness in the air signaled the absence of presence—my isolation in this forbidden corridor of no return. With lingering fear and half-hearted courage I awoke to my destiny, recognized my path. All ultimate journeys must be made alone.

Freedom slips though the mind. I cannot comprehend the vastness of dreams endured and dreams in vain. Time conscious? Time remains. It's now that destiny is shaped. Not then—not when the end is near. Not later when you find the time. For there is no future world to lean on. Suddenly it's here and now! A mirror of our fate reflects to those who know: the time has come.

134

Nothing moved in the darkness of the passage. It was void, and a void meant nothing was there. Both my companions had somehow vanished without trace, leaving me alone to confront my nemesis beyond the West Walls. I called out into the blackness but heard only an answering echo. What's more, the echo didn't seem to be mine. I was isolated without vision and so I hesitated to proceed. I knew that once I began I could never return. But I didn't want to return. It didn't seem to matter, and so I moved down the passage toward the still fading echo.

As I wandered through the darkness I wondered what had happened. That they had abandoned me was out of the question, and the thought of something causing their disappearance sent shivers down my spine. Despite my rational acceptance of destiny, the fear of some lurking danger quickened my pace until eventually I was running, blind to all caution.

It seemed I had been running for hours, having certainly penetrated far beyond the West Walls, when suddenly a brightness appeared in the distance, signaling an exit from this corridor of no return. Was it imagination? Was it illusion? Focusing upon the light eventually brought me to a side opening through which daylight shone the brightness of the outdoors. It was a welcome relief to the dark and lonely confinement.

Out in the sunlit world hundreds of people were scattered about an immense garden park enclosed by stone walls. So this was where the Structural inhabitants were hiding. Some were wandering about while others clustered in small groups. What struck me was their uniformity in wearing the same shabby, gray rags. Though obviously the consequence of their hastily unprepared departure, the impression was one of dismal drudgery.

They seemed to be rehearsing—gesticulating and speaking with grandiloquent affectation. It was a performance, but of what play? Who were the actors, and where was the audience? I jumped down to investigate, landing in the midst of an enactment which unsettled my nerves. Yet there was nowhere else to go, for the performance was everywhere. As I observed the curious play every word and every gesture were predictably anticipated. The writer of the script was obviously a dullard, for the play was in the mundane, soap-opera tradition.

I soon grew bored by the tedious dialogue and lack of excitement. I was just about to leave when the action commenced. An actor suddenly jumped onto the pathway and attacked a passer-by. He knocked her down, grabbed her purse, then stabbed her twice before running away. Her screams of pain were the most realistic performance of the play, but as she continued to cry out long after the scene had ended, I rushed over to investigate the cause of her distress. She was writhing in anguish, her white dress soaked and splattered in blood. It was the most hideous form of amusement I had ever seen. I bent down and cradled her in my arms. I called out for help, but no one else responded.

"She's dying!" I screamed, but the other actors simply continued their performance. "Damn you!" I shouted. "This is no game. She's hurt. She needs a doctor." But even those who saw the blood ignored it as though it were part of the play.

I realized that I would have to run for help. I scanned my direction and was just about to leave when her body suddenly tensed, then slowly relaxed into insensate oblivion. Her iris-blue eyes bulged out in horror. I was revolted, but eventually forced myself to close them forever. It was then I saw that upon her hand, fastened to her finger, she wore a blue crystal ring which sparkled and glowed.

This was no play. These weren't actors playing roles, but simply the aberrated residents of an insane asylum. And here I thought the Madman had been mad! Compared to them the Madman was quite sane. Mixed up in their own crazy worlds, it was no wonder they were unaffected by such a murder—an outrage committed publicly before their eyes. Wandering about made me witness to their pathetic dream-world of make-believe. One man was acting cool. One was acting smart. One responsible. An old, ugly woman was pretending to be beautiful and young. Another was feigning motherhood to a small, stuffed dog. Repulsed by such madness I hurried off through the asylum grounds. But there was no escape, for we were all locked in together.

Two businessmen dressed in the shabby clothing of the asylum sat upon wooden crates bickering over some transaction. Seeing my approach they hastily covered their valuables, but not before I noticed that they were dealing in play money. As I wandered off they once again resumed their argument, becoming so heated that they eventually broke out into a brawl. Both inmates went tumbling over the grass, beating each other with kicks and punches. Off to the side another inmate surreptitiously gathered up the play money and stole quietly away. Following the garden path I noticed a man and a woman playing house with tables and chairs on the lawn.

"Do you know what your son did today?" she screeched as he entered through the imaginary door. "He shattered the bedroom window while playing ball!"

The man grew red with indignation. He unstrapped his leather belt and strode over to the highchair where a stuffed doll sat mindless of its peril. He raised his arm and brought the belt down with a resounding crack across its smiling face. Again and again he whipped the toy until the covering actually tore, releasing a cloud of furry stuffing with each enraged blow. On glancing up he suddenly noticed my presence.

"Mind your own business!" he called out with a sneer. "Unless you want some of this for yourself."

I shook my head in dismay. While leaving I heard a mumbled vulgarity followed by the cracking of the belt as he resumed the discipline. Eventually I came upon a mock battle—grown men playing with toy guns in a make-believe war. It was absurd. Hiding behind trees and crawling through the grass the grown-up children pretended to fight.

"Bang!" they shouted. "Bang! Bang! You're dead!"

The commanders in the background could be seen deploying their armies. The pleasure they received from controlling the movement was evident by their air of superiority and smugness. The entire spectacle was simply ludicrous.

"Get down!" shouted a voice through the clamor of the battle. I turned to see a soldier motioning me to take cover. "Those devils will kill you!" he exclaimed in warning.

"Bang! You're dead!" shouted a voice sneaking up from behind.

I turned to see a toy gun barreling down upon the other soldier's back. Seeing that he had been shot he clutched his heart and fell writhing to the ground. The enemy soldier rushed off for more fun and games. I turned to tell my friend that it was all right to get up. But to my amusement he insisted on playing dead, lying limp and lifeless upon the ground. Grabbing an arm to help him up I recoiled at the sight of a bloodied hole in his back!

I departed the scene as quickly as possible and lost myself in the crowds. Each player was involved in his own make-believe world, each one playing his own little game. None of them had any knowledge of what was actually happening or where they actually were. Concerned with their own petty affairs they only wanted to be left alone. Each of them was so caught up in his own madness that nothing else made any sense. Nothing mattered but the security and comfort of each one's own private domain.

As I made my way through the asylum grounds I noticed a strange figure standing off to the side. It seemed impossible. Was he old or was he young? Did his age even matter? But as I worked my way closer there was no room for doubt.

"Katon!" But he remained motionless with the same vacant expression upon his face. "Katon!" I pleaded while shaking him violently. But it was of no use, for his mind was void, his soul no longer aware. No longer did he recognize my form. No longer did he respond to my call. For him the world had ceased its frenzy. Sounds and voices had lost all meaning, saturating his mind in an incoherent medium of noise. It was his living death, and no one could touch him. No one could begin to understand his way and his world, for he was no longer present. He was living in another dimension, a dimension to which this world is only a dream, a passing phantom that would soon be gone.

A calm, gray silence enters your soul. Nothing matters in the vastness of time and space. Standing passively, acted upon, but not acting upon, turned in circles, moved and touched, you stand and wait for eternity . . . Stand there, let the world go by, let the people walk by not noticing why you just stand and wait, patiently as time passes by and nothing becomes—eternity.

"Come on!" shouted someone grabbing my arm. "Let's get out of here!" Half dazed I turned to see the Professor's Assistant urging me on through the crowd.

"What's wrong?" I asked, finally coming to my senses. "What's happening?"

He seemed strangely uneasy as he glanced about. "We've got to get out of here," he said in fear. Normally calm and rational, his nervousness became contagious. "We must leave before it's too late, before they discover who we are."

But the noisy garden suddenly grew silent. The inmates dropped what they were doing, gazing like zombies at our movement across the grounds. Then all at once they burst forth in pursuit.

"This way!" he called out, motioning to the high, stone wall.

It was a nightmare from which I would surely awaken, shouldn't I? But taking no chance I followed without protest with the sounds of the chase closing in from behind. The Professor's Assistant bent beside the wall, interlacing both hands and boosting me to the top. I then reached down, giving him a hand, and began pulling him up the wall. But it was too late! One of the inmates had grabbed his feet. The Professor's Assistant kicked wildly at his foe, but eventually other inmates grabbed hold and began pulling him down the wall. Holding on till the end, for I couldn't abandon him, I was losing my grip and was being inched over the wall. As more inmates joined the struggle the inevitable occurred and I lost my hold. I fell headfirst into the collapsing pile of bodies. My head crushed painfully against flesh and bone. In an instant the world became black and silent. I had returned to the Asylum in a most undignified manner.

Knowing that I was unconscious, I was at a loss to explain why I was still conscious. I was fully aware of what had just taken place. After sustaining that fall I was certainly knocked out or perhaps even dead. Was this the afterlife? And, if so, what came before? In any case, all I knew was that I was still conscious. I tried to move, but nothing happened. I tried to speak, but there was no sound. Then off in the distance I sensed something happening. Not something just starting up, but something that was taking place all along, as though only now, after taking that fall, was I becoming aware of manifestations on a subliminal plane of existence. Straining my ears I could make out weird and uncanny noises. Inhuman voices and sounds of struggle droned through the air. A peculiar buzzing sensation flowed through my body. My arms and legs began vibrating beyond control. My lips and mouth were buzzing into numbness. Something was happening. Something terrible was about to take place. The world began swirling in uncontrollable frenzy.

"GET THAT FROG!" screamed a hollow voice.

The Adventures of Duckling
MADNESS INCARNATE

———————————————

A SUBLIMINAL PROJECTIONS PRESENTATION

DREAMS INCORPORATED

"GET THAT FROG!" shrieked an inhuman voice. "Get that frog and stuff it down his mouth!"

Duckling could not bear what was happening, for after all, he was just a duck. Duckling's mother pinned him to the ground with her wings, forcing a small frog down his throat, shoving the slimy, squirming body in with her beak. Duckling gagged and coughed to no avail, for the wiggling, green creature was soon slithering down his throat. Duckling was sickened by the vileness of what had happened. Even now he could feel the animal struggling about within his stomach, fighting for one more moment of life.

Satisfied with a job well-done, Duckling's mother waddled off to join her brood of nestlings for a swim. Duckling was ashamed and offended over the indecency of the incident. With tearful indignation he watched from shore as his family swam joyfully about. They dunked their heads occasionally, surfacing with a small fish or tadpole, swallowing it with a slight toss of the head. Duckling knew inwardly that this was not his home, that this was not really his family, for nothing about the world made him feel he belonged. He was horrified by the murder and violence, the perversion of creatures devouring one another for daily nourishment. Everything about the world made him feel a stranger to life. Even his own mother seemed cold and brutal, and it was clear that she favored the rest of her brood over this miserable misfit of an offspring, an outcast weakling who caused her such trouble. Duckling felt lonely and unwanted, yet at the same time he was revolted by a world too dreadful to endure. Why wish to be partner to such horror?

Duckling clearly remembered his first journey into the world. It was then that he first sensed something was amiss. Following their mother away from the nest, the tiny fledglings were led to the edge of the marsh. There the mother duck flopped into the water, followed by her children who, one by one, dropped into the lake. Frightened by the body of dark, murky water, Duckling was baffled by the family's confidence in throwing themselves into its depths. Yet each one leapt into the water without hesitation, held miraculously on its unstable surface like tiny puffballs in the wind.

Eventually it was Duckling's turn, and after much vacillation and prodding he jumped headlong into the lake. With a splash he found himself submerged in the liquid, his gangly limbs and awkward, flailing body having no resistance for keeping him afloat. Down went Duckling farther and farther into the suffocating depths. Trying to scream for help only sent mouthfuls of water down his throat. His lungs were bursting, yet as much as he struggled he failed to reach the surface. Duckling thought he would die when suddenly a large beak yanked him out into the air and onto the shore. Duckling was overjoyed by the rescue only to find himself pulled from one nightmare and plunged into another, for his mother was scolding him severely for his failure, slapping him from side to side with sharp whacks of her beak. Frightened and humiliated, not to mention painful physical abuse, Duckling resolved, then and there, that one day he would leave and never return.

But the days passed quickly and the right moment never seemed to come. It was easy to become habituated to despair. Deep down Duckling knew it was all the same. No matter where he went nothing would ever change, for the same brutality, the same struggle for survival ruled the entire world. At least here he was temporarily safe. At least here he would be protected, if not from harsh punishment, then at least from the horror of being murdered. In this way Duckling compromised his fear and sorrow, resigning himself to a life of bitter humiliation.

Duckling was bewildered by his family's resentment. He never did anything to them, and yet they hated him. Was he a shameful embarrassment? His brothers and sisters teased and taunted him with dirty tricks. And his mother not only allowed it but she beat on him constantly, supposedly all for his own good. Such was the torment Duckling endured until finally he'd had enough. The indignity of having a living creature forced down his throat was too much to bear. It was a wonder that he had even remained this long. Teary-eyed Duckling turned from the shore and pushed his way through the grass. But soon a furious clatter from the lake told him his mother was in pursuit. Obviously she had quickly understood his intentions and was dead set on thwarting his escape. So, he was a prisoner as well. He would see about that. Duckling rushed through the grass jungle as fast as his little, webbed feet would carry him, but soon a thumping of the ground and a thrashing through the grass told him that his mother was close behind. Duckling's heart throbbed in fear of being caught. He no longer cared about freedom, but simply corporal punishment. It was a living nightmare for Duckling—the same nightmare that had haunted him all through his life, a nightmare which was now coming true!

His skinny, little legs ran like mad, but eventually the inevitable occurred and Duckling was caught. His mother prodded him back through the marsh, kicking and shoving, jabbing with her beak and nipping along the way. On reaching the shore Duckling was jeered at by his siblings who joined in the punishment with snaps and thrusts. Suddenly, before he knew it, he was pushed and pulled into the lake! Duckling was convinced that it was only a dream. It couldn't be true. And yet slowly and surely his spindly body and awkward, flailing limbs sank beneath the cold, smothering water. As he struggled to the surface it was Duckling's own survival which forced him to grab his mother's tail feather. With the punishment accomplished he was certain he would be taken ashore, but to Duckling's horror he was being pulled farther out onto the lake! His mother was taking him farther into ever-deepening water, and yet Duckling could not release his hold. Duckling screamed for help, but his brothers and sisters only laughed. "Sink or swim!" they quacked out in amusement.

Duckling was horrified by the undulating body of water. Wave after wave splashed into his face as he was drawn helplessly towards his doom. Gazing downwards Duckling was terrified by the moving shadows. The mere thought of all those lingering creatures nearly drove him insane. He pleaded for mercy, promising never again to escape, but his words were ignored, for Duckling's mother was intent on teaching him to swim.

"It's the way of the world. Sink or swim," she remarked coldly as she pushed him away.

Panic-stricken, Duckling lashed about to stay afloat, but it was of no use, for eventually he lost strength and was pulled into the smothering depths. It won't be long, thought Duckling to himself. It won't be long before she'll dive down in rescue. But the time seemed suspended, and no one appeared— no one but the monsters that glided about, encircling their prey. His lungs bursting for release, Duckling sank farther into the unknown. With fiendish grins the nightmares followed in pursuit, preparing leisurely for the kill. "It's murder!" cried Duckling. "I'm being murdered . . ." he cried out as awareness faded, his soul and spirit succumbing to shock.

Chapter Eight:
A CONSTRUCT OF MY MIND

---

*"The only people I love," the Madman
lamented, "are those I meet in dreams."*

"NO!" I CRIED OUT in the darkness. "Stop it!" I screamed, thrashing about in the void.

"Wake up," whispered a woman's soft and comforting voice. "You're having a nightmare."

A young nurse in a rainbow-colored dress was sitting patiently by the bed, calmly observing my struggle to consciousness.

"What's happening?" I asked, shaken and chilled by a cold, clammy sweat.

"It was only a bad dream," she explained with cheerful, blue eyes. "But it's over now. You were ill, but now you've finally recovered."

"But where am I?" I asked in bewilderment. "How did I get here?"

"I was out on a field trip searching for a chrysalis when, to my utter surprise, there you were lying unconscious in the snow. Apparently you had been roaming aimlessly for some direction. I could tell by your tracks that you had become lost when you finally succumbed to the cold. You were half dead from exposure and delirious with fever, but we're home now and everything will be all right."

"You brought me here yourself?" I asked in disbelief over her frail and slender body.

"It wasn't so hard," she remarked modestly, "for you were asleep at the time."

"Then it was only a dream?" I asked hopefully.

"Yes," she replied. "It was all simply a dream."

With relief I rose from bed and staggered into the living room. Though I failed to recall the circumstances, some strange sense told me I had been here before. Was it in a dream? Was it in my past? I wandered onto the balcony porch and noticed a menagerie of glass jars containing half-open cocoons.

"You shouldn't be out here," she warned as she followed me onto the balcony. "You're still feverish. You'll catch your death of cold." She then noticed my fascination with her glass asylum. "It was such a sight," she remarked as she reminisced over the spectacle. "Hundreds of butterflies all emerging at the same time—bright, rainbow colors glistening in the sunlight, fanning their wings and fluttering about." Then suddenly her face saddened as she remembered the tragedy. "They had emerged all right, but at the wrong time. In the dead of winter none could possibly survive. They flew off into the west toward the dying sun, almost as if following it for its light and warmth. But exposed prematurely to the hostile elements they must certainly have all perished." Her face suddenly brightened as she glanced upon a solitary cocoon off to the side. "All but this one," she mused as she lifted it gently from the glass. "All but this one emerged and flew away. I wonder if its still alive and metamorphosing," she pondered wistfully, cradling the delicate chrysalis in her hands. "Maybe this one will emerge on time."

I gazed down at the black cocoon and only now

noticed the blue, crystal ring upon her finger. The bright, glittering gem seemed to radiate a life and power of its own. I was mesmerized by a pleasantly soothing warmth emanating from within. Glancing up from the chrysalis she caught my fascination with an enticing smile.

"Who are you?" I asked, knowing very well who she was, but compelled to make certain. Her smile vanished as she gazed off into the sunset. She remained silent, as though she had not heard. The stillness grew ominous. The apprehension was unbearable. Uneasy, dreading her answer, timidly I ventured forth. "Are you Iris?" She averted my penetrating eyes. Some gnawing uncertainty filled me with doubt. Then suddenly I understood but had to ask once more. "Who are you?"

Her face saddened. Her body drained of life as she answered slowly and painfully with tear-clouded eyes—each word sapping her of strength and energy. "A construct," the admission pierced my soul with each word, " . . . of your mind."

* * * * *

Misery of existence. Nightmare realm of endless dreams. Never seeing. Never knowing. Never pausing for a rest—constantly moving on. It's the curse of life! And it would never end . . .

The dream paralyzed my soul, pulling me further into its abysmal depths, absorbing me in an unconscious world of chaos. Yet I had to awaken! I had to stop this mindlessness, this shifting veil of illusion. I shook my head desperately from side to side, trying forcefully to ward off these entrancing visions. Once and for all I had to know what was real! I could no longer play the games which dreams demand. Yet I seemed to be in some kind of trance or daze. I tried desperately to regain control, but my mind continually slipped away, for I could not concentrate. Each time I sustained consciousness only briefly before wandering back through the labyrinthine Structure of illusions. It was not simple exhaustion, but rather some strange sort of delirium. I was delirious with life and it was only now that I understood. Part of my soul fought for identity while another part drifted away, oblivious to the consciousness of my control. Eventually I lost my grasp, my soul succumbing to passive awareness, sinking slowly into the subliminal unknown.

The Continuing Adventures of Stickman
NIGHTMARE QUEST FOR TRUTH

A SUBLIMINAL PROJECTIONS PRESENTATION

DREAMS INCORPORATED

STICKMAN WAS AT A LOSS TO KNOW WHAT TO
DO. HE WAS HERE, THAT MUCH WAS CERTAIN.
BUT WHY WAS HE HERE? STICKMAN HAD NO IDEA
WHO HE WAS OR WHAT HE SHOULD DO. AND AS
FAR AS HE KNEW, NO ONE DID. THEIR LAME
EXPLANATIONS WERE NOTHING BUT BADLY CON-
TRIVED JUSTIFICATIONS FOR AN INVOLUNTARY
EXISTENCE. NO ONE REALLY KNEW WHO HE WAS
OR WHAT HE WAS DOING. NO ONE REALLY KNEW
THE MEANING AND PURPOSE OF LIFE. STICKMAN
REALIZED THE ONLY PERSON THAT COULD
ANSWER THE QUESTION WAS HIMSELF, AND SO
RESOLVING TO FIND THE TRUTH HE PICKED A
COMFORTABLE SPOT AND SAT DOWN TO THINK.

        "WHO AM I," THOUGHT STICKMAN TO
HIMSELF, "AND WHY DO I EXIST?" APPARENTLY
STICKMAN WAS NOT RESPONSIBLE FOR HIS
EXISTENCE, FOR OTHERWISE HE WOULD HAVE NO
NEED TO ASK THE QUESTION. THIS FIRST
CONCLUSION REVOLTED STICKMAN, YET NEVER-
THELESS HE FORCED HIMSELF TO ACCEPT WHAT
HE HAD FELT INWARDLY ALL ALONG--THAT HE
WAS AN EFFECT AND NOT A CAUSE. STICKMAN
WAS NOT A CAUSAL AGENT, BUT SIMPLY AN
EFFECT, A BY-PRODUCT OF SOME PRECONCEIVED
PLAN. HE WAS A LEFTOVER RESULT, ALONE TO
PICK UP THE PIECES AFTER ALL HAD BEEN
SAID AND DONE.

DISGUSTED BY THIS LAST CONCLUSION,
STICKMAN FELT NOTHING BUT CONTEMPT FOR THE
WORLD AROUND HIM. HE DID NOT WISH TO BE A
DUMB IDIOT WITH NO VOICE IN HIS OWN
EXISTENCE. HE DID NOT WISH TO BE A SLAVE
TO SOME ULTERIOR MOTIVE OR POWER. HE
WANTED TO BE HIMSELF, BUT AT PRESENT HE
HAD NO IDEA WHAT THAT SELF COULD BE.
STICKMAN KNEW ONLY THAT SITTING UPON THE
HILL WAS MAKING HIM DROWSY, AND SO HE
LAY BACK TO REST AS THE SUN SET BEHIND
THE WESTERN MOUNTAINS. "WHAT IS REAL?"
THOUGHT STICKMAN TO HIMSELF WHILE DRIFTING
ASLEEP. "WHAT IS REALLY REAL?"

"WHAT WOULD YOU LIKE TO BE REAL?" SAID
A VOICE FROM THE UNKNOWN.

STICKMAN WAS SURPRISED AT FINDING
HIMSELF MATERIALIZING IN ANOTHER DIMENSION.
"PERHAPS," THOUGHT STICKMAN, "PERHAPS NOW
I'LL KNOW THE TRUTH." IT WAS A STAGE
COMPLETELY SURROUNDED BY VOID.

"YES?" ASKED SOMEONE SEATED AT A
DESK. "WHAT IS IT YOU WANT?" CASUALLY
WAITING TO BE OF SERVICE, THE CLERK SAT
PATIENTLY IN A CONDESCENDING, BUSINESSLIKE
MANNER.

"I'M NOT SURE," REPLIED STICKMAN IN A
PUZZLED TONE. "WHAT DO YOU HAVE?"

"ALL SORTS OF THINGS!" THE CLERK
EXCLAIMED, DROPPING HIS OFFICIAL AIR.
"ANYTHING YOU CAN IMAGINE IS NOW WITHIN
YOUR REACH." SPREADING HIS ARMS HE
INDICATED THE PILES OF PAMPHLETS SCATTERED
OVER THE DESK. "FOR EXAMPLE, TAKE THIS
ONE," HE SAID, OPENING A COLORFUL
BROCHURE. "LIFETIME IN PARADISE! EVERY
WISH FULFILLED! EVERYTHING THE WAY
YOU'D LIKE IT!"

"THAT WOULDN'T BE TOO EXCITING,"
THOUGHT STICKMAN, "FOR AFTER AWHILE LIFE
WOULD BECOME BORINGLY PREDICTABLE."

"YOU DON'T UNDERSTAND," EXPLAINED THE
CLERK AS THOUGH READING STICKMAN'S MIND.
"I CAN ARRANGE THINGS ANYWAY YOU'D LIKE.
IF YOU WANT SOME EXCITING EVENTS TO BREAK
THE MONOTONY, THAT CAN BE ARRANGED. IN
FACT, I WON'T EVEN INFORM YOU OF THEM.
THEY'LL BE COMPLETELY UNEXPECTED."

"BUT STILL," STICKMAN REPLIED, "IT
WOULDN'T SEEM RIGHT HAVING EVERYTHING MY
WAY, HAVING EVERY WISH FULFILLED. I
WOULD SOON BECOME SPOILED AND TIRED OF
LIFE."

THE CLERK WAS AMUSED BY THIS INFERIOR
CREATURE, A CREATURE WHO, HAVING THE CHANCE,
WOULD REJECT THE ABILITY TO TRANSFORM THE
WORLD INTO HIS OWN IDEALS. "ALL RIGHT," HE
REPLIED, "THEN HOW ABOUT THIS. EVERY SO
OFTEN I'LL ARRANGE SOME ACCIDENT. HOW
ABOUT A FEW PERSONAL TRAGEDIES? THE DEATH
OF YOUR WIFE OR CHILD? PERHAPS SOME BAD
TIMES AND FINANCIAL DIFFICULTIES TO KEEP
YOU STRUGGLING. AS FREQUENTLY AS YOU'D
LIKE I CAN ARRANGE TO THWART YOUR DESIRES
AND GOALS. YOU CAN MOLD YOUR DESTINY INTO
ANY SHAPE. JUST TELL ME WHAT YOU WANT AND
I'LL MAKE IT COME TRUE." BUT STICKMAN
SIMPLY SHOOK HIS HEAD AND TURNED AWAY.

"WELL THEN HOW ABOUT THIS?" ENQUIRED
THE CLERK AS HE REACHED FOR ANOTHER
PAMPHLET. "TRUE LOVE AT LAST! ETERNAL
ROMANCE WITH ONE WHO CARES--A COMPANION
FOR LIFE. HERE," SAID THE CLERK,
DROPPING THE BOOKLET AND PICKING UP A
PENCIL, "I'LL DRAW HER FOR YOU." AND
ON THE EMPTY SPACE BESIDE STICKMAN HE
DREW THE FIGURE OF A GIRL. "IF YOU
DON'T LIKE THIS ONE," THE CLERK REMARKED,
"I CAN ALWAYS DRAW ANOTHER, OR BETTER
YET, YOU CAN DRAW HER YOURSELF. THINK
OF IT: THE GIRL OF YOUR DREAMS--A
FAITHFUL, CONSIDERATE COMPANION, A
LOVING, YOUNG WIFE TO COMFORT YOU
THROUGH THE YEARS. IT'S OUR MOST
POPULAR REQUEST." BUT STICKMAN ONLY
SHOOK HIS HEAD. AND WITH A SIGH THE
CLERK ERASED THE BEAUTIFUL DRAWING
FOREVER FROM SIGHT.

"WELL, WHAT IS IT YOU'D LIKE?" THE
CLERK ASKED IN EXASPERATION. "MONEY?
POWER? PLEASURE? FAME? YOU CAN HAVE
ANYTHING YOU WANT, BUT FIRST YOU MUST
DECIDE."

"BUT IT SERVES NO PURPOSE," STICKMAN
ARGUED.

"WHOSE PURPOSE?" ASKED THE CLERK.
"YOURS? SOMEONE ELSE'S? THE WORLD'S?
NATURE'S? GOD'S?" PAUSING FOR A MOMENT,
HE MOVED TO THE FAR END OF THE STAGE.
"OVER HERE," HE SAID AS HE BROUGHT
STICKMAN ANOTHER PILE OF PAMPHLETS. "SEE
IF YOU CAN FIND SOMETHING HERE YOU'D
LIKE. AND TAKE YOUR TIME," HE ADDED AS
STICKMAN GLANCED HASTILY THROUGH THE
PILE. "FOR YOU HAVE ALL THE TIME IN THE
WORLD."

STICKMAN OPENED A BOOKLET ENTITLED,
IN THE SERVICE OF GOD, AND BEGAN SCANNING
THE TABLE OF CONTENTS.

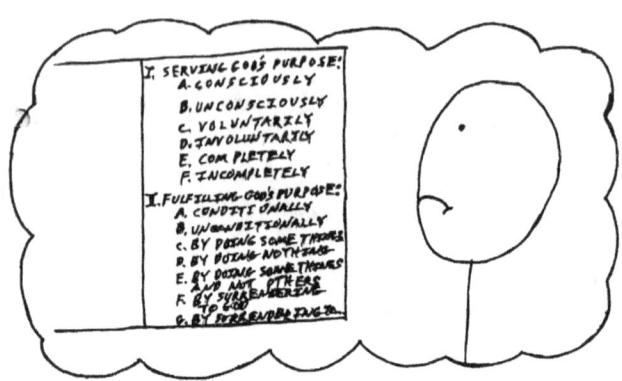

"NOTHING QUITE SUIT YOUR TASTE?"
ENQUIRED THE CLERK AS STICKMAN RETURNED
THE PILE OF PAMPHLETS. "I HAVE MANY MORE
WHERE THOSE CAME FROM."

STICKMAN SHOOK HIS HEAD IN DISGUST.
"I DON'T WANT TO SERVE ANYONE ELSE'S
PURPOSE. I WANT TO SERVE MY OWN!"

"WELL, WHAT IS YOUR PURPOSE?" ASKED
THE CLERK. "WHAT IS IT YOU WANT?"

"I DON'T KNOW," STICKMAN CONFESSED
WITH SHAME. "I HONESTLY DON'T KNOW."

"WELL THEN I CAN'T HELP YOU," REPLIED
THE CLERK, AND SLOWLY THE DREAM BEGAN
FADING INTO DARKNESS. STICKMAN TRIED
DESPERATELY TO RETAIN THE VISION, BUT
GRADUALLY IT SLIPPED FROM REACH.

"ALL I WANT TO KNOW," HE CALLED OUT
IN DESPAIR, "IS WHAT'S REAL!"

"REAL?" ECHOED THE VOICE FROM THE
UNKNOWN. "YOU WANT TO KNOW WHAT'S REAL?"
IT MOCKED WITH AWFUL LAUGHTER. "THE
PROFESSOR," IT MANAGED TO BLURT OUT
BETWEEN LAUGHS. "FIND THE PROFESSOR,"
SAID THE VOICE OVER AND OVER AS THE
DREAM FADED INTO SILENCE.

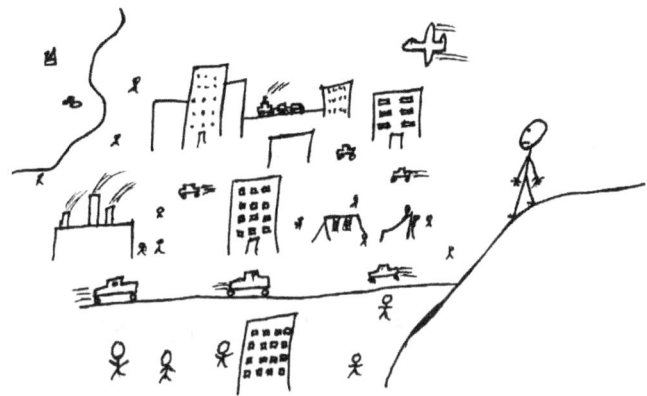

WHEN THE MORNING DAWNED STICKMAN
LOOKED AT THE WORLD--THE COMMOTION OF
GAMES AND ILLUSIONS. BUT WITH THE MEMORY
OF THE DREAM IT NO LONGER MATTERED.
BECAUSE A ROCK IS HARD AND STAGNANT ALL
IT CAN DO IS WEATHER AWAY. AND SO, TOO,
THESE PEOPLE HE SAW. FOR EACH MAN IS
EQUAL TO HIS DESTINY. AND ALL THEIR
DESTINIES ARE LIKE THE PAGES OF A BOOK,
OR LIKE THE ROCKS FOR WHICH ONLY TIME
CAN WEATHER AWAY. STICKMAN'S DREAM THIS
MORNING DAWNED, AND LEFT ONLY THE RUINS
OF EMPTINESS.

STICKMAN SEARCHED EVERYWHERE FOR THE PROFESSOR, BUT HE WAS NOWHERE AROUND. NO ONE HAD EVEN HEARD OF THE PROFESSOR, MUCH LESS KNEW OF HIS WHEREABOUTS. TIRED AND DEPRESSED, STICKMAN CONTINUED THE SEARCH, AND SLOWLY THE MEMORY OF HIS DREAM CAME TO MIND.

"WAS IT POSSIBLE?" HE THOUGHT. "IN REAL LIFE COULD IT POSSIBLY BE TRUE?" AND SUDDENLY STICKMAN KNEW EXACTLY WHAT TO DO. FINDING A PENCIL HE LOCATED THE NEAREST BLANK PAGE AND BEGAN TO DRAW.

"YES?" ASKED THE VOICE AS SOON AS
STICKMAN WAS DONE. "WHAT IS IT YOU WANT?"
"THAT'S WHAT I WANT TO KNOW!"
EXCLAIMED STICKMAN IN DESPAIR. "I DON'T
KNOW WHO I AM OR WHY I'M HERE! I DON'T
KNOW WHERE I CAME FROM OR WHERE I'M GOING!
I DON'T KNOW WHAT'S TRUE OR WHAT'S AN
ILLUSION! HOW CAN I KNOW WHAT I WANT WHEN
I DON'T EVEN KNOW WHAT'S REAL?"

"FIRST OF ALL," THE PROFESSOR CALMLY
REPLIED, "LET'S START FROM THE BEGINNING.
YOU SAY THAT YOU DON'T KNOW WHY YOU'RE
HERE, BUT DO YOU KNOW WHERE HERE IS?"

"HERE IS HERE," ARGUED STICKMAN.
"I'M HERE. YOU'RE HERE. EVERYTHING IS
HERE."

"YES," AGREED THE PROFESSOR. "BUT ARE
YOU SURE HERE IS WHAT IT APPEARS TO BE?
YOU YOURSELF ADMIT THAT YOU DON'T KNOW
WHAT'S REAL. HOW DO YOU KNOW THAT HERE IS
REALLY HERE? PERHAPS HERE IS REALLY THERE,
IN WHICH CASE YOUR QUESTION SHOULD BE
REPHRASED: WHY AM I THERE? OR PERHAPS
HERE IS ONLY AN ILLUSION, IN WHICH CASE
YOUR QUESTION SHOULD BE: WHY DOES HERE
APPEAR?"

STICKMAN WAS BAFFLED BY THE MENTAL
GYMNASTICS. "WELL WHAT'S THE POINT?"

"THE POINT IS," SAID THE PROFESSOR,
"THAT YOU HAVE NO IDEA WHAT HERE IS."

"I SUPPOSE NOT," ACKNOWLEDGED
STICKMAN. "I ALWAYS THOUGHT THAT HERE WAS
HERE. I ALWAYS THOUGHT THAT THINGS WERE
WHAT THEY WERE." BUT THE PROFESSOR ONLY
SMILED IN DISAGREEMENT.

"YOU SEE," HE EXPLAINED, "ULTIMATELY
EVERYTHING IS OF A QUESTIONABLE NATURE,
ESPECIALLY THOSE THINGS OVER WHICH WE HAVE
NO CONTROL."

"FOR EXAMPLE," CONTINUED THE PROFESSOR
AS THEY FOUND THEMSELVES ON THE NEXT PAGE,
"LOOK AROUND AND TELL ME WHAT YOU SEE."

STICKMAN SURVEYED THE LANDSCAPE AND
REPORTED HIS FINDINGS. "THE SUN IS SHINING.
THE TREES ARE GROWING. THE CLOUDS ARE
FLOATING THROUGH THE AIR. AND A DUCKLING
IS FLYING TOWARD THE WESTERN MOUNTAINS."

"TRUE," SAID THE PROFESSOR, "BUT IS IT
REAL, AND IS IT HERE?"

"AS FAR AS I KNOW," STICKMAN REPLIED.
"IT APPEARS REAL. AT ANY RATE IT'S ALL
I'VE EVER KNOWN."

THE PROFESSOR PAUSED A MOMENT IN
CONSIDERATION. "IF YOU WANT TO KNOW THE
TRUTH," HE EXPLAINED, "IF YOU WANT TO KNOW
WHERE YOU REALLY ARE THEN WALK FORWARD IN
A STRAIGHT LINE."

THE PROFESSOR'S WORDS GAVE STICKMAN A
FEELING OF UNCERTAINTY, BUT SLOWLY AND
SURELY HE MOVED TOWARD THE EDGE OF THE
PAGE.

    "NO!" SHOUTED THE PROFESSOR. "YOU'RE
NOT FOLLOWING A STRAIGHT PATH!" STICKMAN
HAD INDEED VEERED FAR FROM COURSE, CURVING
SHARPLY TO THE LEFT TOWARD THE WESTERN
MOUNTAINS.

    "I'M GOING STRAIGHT!" STICKMAN
COUNTERED IN DISBELIEF, BUT ON SEEING HIS
POSITION HE CONCEDED THE ERROR, RETURNED
TO THE START AND BEGAN ONCE MORE.

    "YOU'RE HEADING LEFT AGAIN!" THE
PROFESSOR CALLED OUT. "MOVE MORE TO THE
RIGHT!" BUT THIS TIME STICKMAN OVER-
COMPENSATED AND VEERED SHARPLY TO THE
RIGHT. "TOO FAR!" SHOUTED THE PROFESSOR.
AND ONCE AGAIN STICKMAN RETURNED FOR
ANOTHER TRY.

STICKMAN WAS BAFFLED BY HIS INABILITY
TO WALK STRAIGHT. HE PROCEEDED SLOWLY TO
OBSERVE THE PHENOMENON AND EVENTUALLY
DETECTED A SLIGHT PULL TOWARD THE LEFT.
AS HE COMPENSATED FOR THE PULL AND
CONTINUED FORWARD AN EQUALLY PERSUASIVE
FORCE NOW PULLED HIM TO THE RIGHT.
STICKMAN WAS ASTONISHED BY THIS SUBLIMINAL
POWER WHICH HAD UNKNOWINGLY AFFECTED HIM
ALL THROUGH HIS LIFE. COMPENSATING FOR
THE RIGHT PULL HE SLOWLY PRESSED FORWARD
WHEN SUDDENLY IT CHANGED AGAIN TO THE LEFT.
BACK AND FORTH THE FORCES ALTERNATED LIKE
SOME GHOSTLY GAME OF TUG-OF-WAR, AND THE
MORE HE RESISTED, THE MORE PERSISTENT THEY
BECAME, GROWING STEADILY STRONGER WITH EACH
STEP OF THE WAY. IT WAS LIKE SOME
INVISIBLE FORCE FIELD MARKING THE
BOUNDARIES OF ANOTHER WORLD, A SECRET WORLD
WHICH STICKMAN WAS DETERMINED TO ENTER.
STICKMAN BATTLED TO MAINTAIN A STRAIGHT
COURSE AND FINALLY BROKE THROUGH TO THE
EDGE OF THE PAGE.

"THERE'S NOTHING HERE!" STICKMAN CRIED
IN ALARM AS HE PEERED CAUTIOUSLY OVER THE
EDGE OF THE PAGE. IT WAS VOID. AND ONLY
DARKNESS AND SILENCE MET STICKMAN'S GAZE.
"IT'S EMPTY!" HE GASPED. "THERE'S NOTHING
BEYOND." STICKMAN RUSHED FRANTICALLY ALONG
THE FOUR SIDES OF THE PAGE. "IT'S A SQUARE!"
HE SCREAMED. "I'VE LIVED MY LIFE ON A
SQUARE FLOATING IN THE MIDDLE OF NOTHINGNESS!
AND NONE OF IT'S REAL," HE BEMOANED ON
TOUCHING THE DRAWINGS OF TREES AND
MOUNTAINS. "NONE OF IT HAS ANY SUBSTANCE."
"YOU'RE ON A PAGE," EXPLAINED THE
PROFESSOR. "YOU'RE ON A PAGE IN A BOOK,
AN ABSURDLY STRUCTURED BOOK WITH A MADMAN
FOR AN AUTHOR. AND YOU YOURSELF ARE ONLY
A CHARACTER IN AN UNFINISHED STORY. DO YOU
WANT TO SEE YOURSELF AS YOU REALLY ARE?"
AND ON THE NEXT PAGE A MIRROR WAS DRAWN
BEFORE STICKMAN.

STICKMAN STOOD PETRIFIED BEFORE THE
MIRROR. FOR ONCE HE SAW HIMSELF AS HE REALLY
WAS: A CHILDISH HODGEPODGE OF STICKS AND
LINES. STICKMAN WAS HORRIFIED BY THE ABSURD,
LITTLE CREATURE WITHIN THE MIRROR. IT
COULDN'T BE TRUE! HE KNEW THE REFLECTION
COULDN'T BE HIMSELF, AND YET STANDING BEFORE
HIM WAS A PREPOSTEROUS IMAGE WHICH MOCKED
HIS EVERY MOVEMENT.

"THIS IS WHAT YOU REALLY ARE," EXPLAINED
THE PROFESSOR. "A STICKMAN WITH NO MEANING
OR PURPOSE, LIVING IN A MAKE-BELIEVE WORLD
OF NO VALUE OR ESSENCE. THERE'S NOTHING
MORE TO KNOW, NOTHING MORE TO FIND. YOUR
LIFE HAS BEEN PLOTTED OUT AND THE STORY LINE
HAS BEEN SET. YOU WILL CONTINUE THROUGH TO
THE END OF THE CHAPTER AND THEN DIE AN
UNAVOIDABLY PAINFUL DEATH. NOTHING MORE
AWAITS YOU. NOTHING MORE CAN BE SAID. FOR
YOU ARE SIMPLY A COMIC-BOOK REPRESENTATION--
AN ABSURD CARICATURE IN THE SIMPLEST FORM."

STICKMAN WENT INSANE. IN ONE STROKE
HIS WORLD HAD LOST ALL REALITY. IN ONE
STROKE HIS VERY BEING WAS TORN ASUNDER BY
THE TRUTH. STICKMAN RUSHED HYSTERICALLY
ABOUT THE PAGE, YET THERE WAS NOWHERE TO GO
AND NOTHING TO DO. THERE WAS NO MEANING
AND NO PURPOSE. THE WHOLE WORLD WAS
NOTHING BUT A TRAGIC FARCE, A STUPID GAME
WHERE HAPPENSTANCE RULES. STICKMAN WAS
TRAPPED IN A NIGHTMARE WITH NO CHANCE OF
AWAKENING. HE RANTED AND RAVED LIKE A
MANIAC, THRASHING ABOUT IN SPIRITUAL
TORMENT. THEN SUDDENLY HE GLANCED UP AND
SAW ME GAZING DOWN UPON THE PAGE.

"YOU!" HE SCREAMED ACCUSINGLY. "YOU
DID THIS TO ME! YOU'RE RESPONSIBLE FOR
IT ALL!" AND SUDDENLY HE WENT BESERK IN
FRUSTRATION AND REVENGE. "I'LL KILL YOU!"
HE SCREAMED OVER AND OVER. AND WITH ONE
BOUND HE LEAPT OFF THE SIDE OF THE PAGE . . .

There was a thump. It couldn't be real, yet I had no time for thought, for right beside me was the clatter of Stickman rising to his feet. I dropped the book and ran for my life.

"This can't be happening," I told myself, but the growing clatter of Stickman's pursuit convinced me of the horror.

"I'll kill you!" he screamed. His demonic laughter echoed throughout the dark stage, sending an icy chill running up my spine.

"This can't be real," I blubbered, shaking my head frantically in a futile effort to awake. But it was real. And it was coming to get me. "Life is nice," I chanted to myself. "Life is nice. I have no qualms. Life is nice. I have no qualms." Running blindly across the stage I was on the point of collapse when suddenly the floor gave way, plunging me into the void. I remembered nothing but the incessant refrain echoing throughout the empty darkness. But was it true? And was it me? Was life indeed nice? And did I myself really have no qualms? Only darkness and an icy wind answered my descent into the unknown.

Chapter Nine:
HARBINGER OF DEATH

"For we are all insane, and our only possible asylum is within our own illusions . . . We only live and die . . ."

—THE MADMAN

My life is like a nightmare, only much worse, for it is a nightmare I can't awaken from. Nightmare within nightmare, nightmare after nightmare. Each awakening is an awakening into a nightmare. Who can help me? Who can help an illusion?

—THE SUBJECT

The Resurrection of Duckling
NIGHTMARE WITHOUT END

AND THERE WAS NO END. Duckling could not even die without a surviving consciousness. He could not even experience the terror of being murdered without the anguish of continual rebirth. Duckling still remembered his previous life. Painfully he recalled the dreadful world of violence, a world where reality was a living nightmare. Duckling had witnessed the struggle for survival: sentient creatures devouring one another in an endless pursuit of predator and prey. Even the tiniest were engaged in the struggle. It wasn't bad enough that the visible world was filled with brutality, but on every leaf and twig, under every rock, in every hole, nook, and cranny the eternal battle raged on. It wasn't simply the exception, but the overwhelming rule that violence and suffering were an integral part of nature. Famine, disease, destruction, and death all flourished throughout the history of life. Since the dawn of consciousness, senseless pain and horror were the law of nature which ravaged the world. Nature: red in tooth and claw was an apt metaphor.

Duckling could not come to terms with such madness. He shuddered to think that such a world could exist, a world which at any moment should vanish as a nightmare, but which stubbornly persisted as if out of mockery and spite. Duckling had wished to God that it was a dream, that one day he would finally awaken, but day after horrible day was the same and nothing ever faded but his hopes. In time of stress when the tension was unbearable he thought it was over, that all he need do was close his eyes in prayer and open them to a new world, yet he would open them to find the same living nightmare haunting him till the end which never came.

Duckling lived his life on the brink of disaster, goaded by the constant feeling of doom. He had no idea what he was after or where he was going. All he knew was that something was wrong, that somehow he did not belong in this world, that somehow he must escape from the nightmare of his life. His death, as gruesome as it was, had provided that escape—or so Duckling had thought. Instead he found himself re-awakening to a new nightmare, ready once more to resume his tragic role. It was the wheel of life. And it turned in circles. Once more cycling back to the beginning.

And now where was he? Duckling found himself trapped within darkness, entombed alive with no way of escape. Everywhere he turned there was only a smooth, hard surface with no cracks or openings through which to break free. Hemmed in on all sides, Duckling was a prisoner of the void, abandoned to his own living tomb. In claustrophobic terror Duckling struggled for freedom. In panic he hurled himself against the invisible wall. With each blow the universe resounded internally. Each impact sent shock waves reverberating through his mind. Suffocating in darkness, smothering from heat, Duckling struggled for room to breathe. Gasping for air he smashed against the wall until finally, with a cracking and crumbling, he was free! Then suddenly, in one awful moment, Duckling realized what he had done. The eggshell crumbled. The nightmare would begin once more.

* * * * *

How I arrived here, I could not explain. Suffice it to say that I had never known whether I was here or there, or whether I was coming or going. All my life was simply an endless progression of scenes without meaning or consistency, incoherent and irrelevant, passing through, then abandoning me to the darkness and silence. Nightmare after nightmare, one senseless dream after another. I never knew where I was or what came next. I never knew what was real or what merely a dream. And now where was I? Forest wilderness, or only an illusion? Ghostly phantom, or horrifying reality? Yes, I was running—running because I was afraid. Afraid of everyone and everything. Afraid that the moment I stopped would be my doom. I never asked to be here. I never asked to be anywhere. Yet regardless of my feelings I was shuffled from one dream to another, forced to act my part like a puppet on a string.

I found myself lost, thrashing my way through a wilderness of unconscious growth. I was trapped in a nightmare of someone else's imagining. It was not my part to play. I was not responsible for this scenario. Yet nevertheless I was here, and whether I liked it or not I was forced to take part.

"Duckling," said a sly, cunning voice. And slowly and surely I was being dragged into another world. "I'll cut off your head and roast you for dinner," said the evil demon. "Roast Duckling smothered in orange sauce. M-M-M-M-M! Delicious! Already my mouth waters for your tender flesh."

"Pervert!" screamed Duckling. "Evil monster! You'll pay for it in the end!"

"Silly Duckling," said the demon with a fiendish grin. "There is no end . . ."

No end! Of course there was no end. How could there be? How could I have possibly forgotten? Of course I must apologize at once and repent my sins. Bowing down on my knees, lying prostrate before eternity, I must humble myself and pay tribute for such a wonderful life.

"Thank you."

"Thank you, indeed."

And indeed thanks were due. How fortunate I was to live forever. How lucky to be chosen for this paradise. Overcome with joy I cried in happiness at the thought of eternal niceness.

"You mean I'll never have to die?"

"You'll never die."

"And I can have anything I want?"

"Anything you want."

"All the animals I can eat?"

"It shall be provided."

All the games I can play?"

"If that be your bent."

"All the pleasures of the world?"

"For as long as you live."

"Oh, happy days! My life is so nice! Who could ask for anything more?"

I could . . . I could at least request the pounding in my head to cease. That would provide considerable relief. So, too, would the removal of those strange, buzzing voices which never let me rest. Sleep would also be beneficial—a sleep, that is, without those dreams. And if only I could know for sure when I was dreaming. If only I knew that it was all unreal, then at least my mind would be set at ease. But with constant shift from dream to reality to delirium, I never knew what was true. One moment the world was consistently real, and the next moment I was plunged into insanity. One moment the world was peaceful, and the next moment I was assailed by chaos and terror.

"Murderer!" screamed a voice out of nowhere. And in a flash I was assaulted by a wild-eyed maniac. "Murderer!" he cried, pouncing upon me and clawing my neck. Whirling, tossing, and flinging about, the world was a tumult of struggle and confusion. Eventually I managed to wrestle free, sending the lunatic sprawling to the ground.

"Go ahead and kill me!" he pleaded. "It's all over anyway." He collapsed and lay passive, gazing vacantly through and beyond. Life, for him, no longer mattered. "Iris is dead," he moaned. His world had fallen apart, crumbling before him into ashes and dust. "My wife and children are dead," he sobbed. And nothing else made any difference.

He no longer needed a reason to die. It was no longer necessary to justify his death as he had so long justified his life—not to anyone, not even himself. The thought had never crossed his mind. Without hesitation he proceeded forth with what was required, and of what he required. For once he was free and knew exactly what to do. Without reflecting over the consequences, he simply acted—giving no thought to the pain or method involved.

"Now then," said a disaffected voice, "taking a needle, carefully pierce the skin in the region of the lower abdomen and insert far enough to puncture the abdominal cavity. Withdraw the needle and, holding the body between the thumb and forefinger, squeeze gently to expel the contents of the skin. Pressure should first be applied in the lower regions to expel the colon, the intestines, and the stomach, moving progressively upwards into the thorax to expel the heart, the nerve cord, and the brain. After squeezing out all the internal organs and fluids, hold the flaccid skin over heated air to allow it to expand to its original state. Insert a straw or grass stem into the incision and gently inflate with a breath of air. Continue this process until the skin has resumed its natural appearance. The specimen is now ready for mounting."

* * * * *

"Stay away!" screamed a voice. There was no differentiating the source. With a burst of energy I once more willed myself back to consciousness. Running deliriously through the woods I had no idea where I was, or where I was going. All I knew was that I had to keep running, that somehow I had to escape from this merry-go-round of absurdity. And yet there was nowhere to go, for I had already gone too far. I had seen too much, and now I could never return. I was lost in the nightmare of endless illusions. I was trapped forever within the Structural labyrinth of life, doomed to play the fool like a puppet on a string. It was the ultimate insanity, a never-ending cycle of futility. And it made no difference. And it served no end. And I knew at last the truth about life. For there was no meaning. There was no purpose. There was no higher reality. It was simply here. And I was here. And there was nothing I could do but run. Yet there was nowhere to go and nothing to do. It was an eternal farce from beginning to end.

I couldn't breathe. Or was I hyperventilating? My spirit rebelled against the madness of existence. Gasping for air, my heart spasming in pain, I staggered forth and stumbled upon a gruesome sight. "Life is nice," I mumbled disjointedly. "Life is nice. I have no qualms. Life is nice. I have no qualms." And my very being recoiled from the mutilated body of my friend and comrade, the Professor's Assistant. It were as though some devastating force had literally ripped him apart. Splattered blood stained the leaves and grass a bright red. Dismembered, half-eaten arms and legs lay scattered over the ground like so many chunks of meat. His mangled body was torn to shreds, revealing slimy guts which oozed slowly to the ground. And on top of all this he was still alive! Fresh blood spurted from the open wounds in the rhythmically pulsating bursts of an ever-fading life. He was oblivious to what was happening. His shocked face was that of a frightened child who has no idea what he has done.

The nauseating sight made me vomit from the depths of my soul. It was life itself which was being disgorged—a sickening, souring, regurgitated mass of indigestion. "You're killing him!" I pleaded for mercy. Perhaps somehow, someway, the nightmare would end before its fatal conclusion. Perhaps somewhere some merciful force would hear me and intervene. And yet nothing changed. He was dying, and nothing could save him. His face was turning white as each moment more and more of his precious blood pumped and spewed forth onto the ground. Dropping to my knees I grabbed the bloody trunk of his body, shaking him in order to make him understand. "Wake up!" I screamed. "Wake up before it's too late!" But it was already too late. He had gone too far and he could never return. To die in a dream meant dying in real life. Whatever that was.

He was indifferent to my presence. He didn't seem to know me. His vacant eyes gazed through and beyond. It no longer mattered to him one way or another. Life or death. Reality or illusion. It made no difference, for it was all the same. He was indifferent now. He no longer cared about the world and all its petty problems. He no longer cared about reality or the search for truth, for he had long since realized that they were all an illusion. Life was an illusion. The world was an illusion. There was no reality but the reality of illusions. And there was no meaning or purpose to existence. There was no meaning or purpose to anything. For it was all a comedy. A senseless inanity. An eternal joke without beginning or end. Tired and disillusioned, he realized only now that he cared about nothing, not about people or ideas, nor of dreams or goals, nor of anything and everything he could imagine. He only knew that he was tired of life, so tired that he simply lay down to die.

"Murderers!" I screamed in hatred. And I hated it all. Was this all there was to life? Had I journeyed this far only to end in madness? How could this be? I couldn't believe that it was happening. But it was true. Reality was unfolding before my eyes, and there was nothing there—nothing but a void of indifference—a vacuum reality of insignificance.

A sudden piercing scream rent the air, tearing the very fabric of existence. The resonating cry went echoing through the woods, and it was only now that I realized it was mine. I stood motionless as the living world froze in dead silence. Everything seemed to be watching and waiting. Every living creature seemed to be lying in wait. The stillness in the air held an ominous feeling of dread, a feeling that something was about to occur. It was a sadistic prelude to a living nightmare come true. Yet it was real, and it was actually taking place. I was trembling in apprehension when a sudden rustling of the grass told me that the nightmare had already begun.

I was running, running as I had always run, throughout my dreams, throughout my life. The nightmare was moving closer, droning through my mind, pulsing through the forest in anticipation of death. "It isn't real," I repeated over and over, trying to convince myself that it was only a dream. But it was real. It was coming to get me. And I was running for my life, thrashing and flailing, stumbling my way over the forest floor. The world reeled. My body was soaked with the clamminess of death. "Stop it!" I screamed. But the terrible throbbing grew louder, resounding through the air like the heartbeat of madness. Glancing back I saw a monstrous demon lashing its way through the undergrowth. Each moment the living nightmare was growing closer. Each moment I was that much closer to death. The vision of grisly dismemberment flashed through my mind. Was this it? Was this the completion of the cycle? Was this my destiny—to be devoured alive? The thought made me frantic. Had I come this far, traveled all these years, only to serve as food for some fiendish beast? Was all my life nothing but a preparation for this hideous death? My heart throbbed! My head droned! The world swirled in a frenzied daze.

"Iris!—Katon!—Save me!" I cried. But it was of no use, for there was no one there. No one answered, for I was trapped alone, as I was destined alone. The pounding increased. The sounds of pursuit drew near. It was the end. I was about to die. My entire life amounted to nothing. For there was nothing—nothing but madness and horror and pain and brutality.

"Bang!—Bang!" I screamed. "Bang! Bang!— Bang! Bang!" But a sudden lunge from behind sent me sprawling to the ground. Dazed by the fall, I struggled impotently against a demon of claws and teeth. "NO!-!-!" I screamed as a searing pain slashed through my face. And in one stroke the razor claws had torn out half my sight! In one stroke I was maimed and disfigured for life! My eye burned as though it were on fire. Blood poured from the open wound like streams of agonizing tears. "Life is nice," I cried for mercy, scrambling about for some way to escape. But another gashing pain suddenly burned through my leg, tearing and chewing till it ripped out a chunk of raw flesh, my flesh! My body convulsed. My teeth ground in torment, crushing together, crackling and crumbling like pieces of chalk. I couldn't take any more. But I was forced to take more. Once again the searing pain tore through my leg, crunching through to the very marrow of my bones. Half-conscious, delirious with pain, I was too shocked to do anything but endure the torture. It was tearing me apart! Clawing! Ripping! Slashing through muscles and flesh! Gnawing and pulling at nerves and tendons till they suddenly snapped free, leaving me dismembered for life. I should have passed out from the torment, but the sadistic force held me conscious till the end. My teeth were ground to tiny fragments. My eye was burning with bloody tears. Horribly disfigured. Crippled and maimed. My entire leg was wrenched from its socket, lying hideously detached like an alien form no longer mine.

"I'll kill you!" I cried out in anguish. Struggling to my knee I saw the demon feasting upon my dismembered leg. "Murderer!" I screamed while grabbing the nearest solid branch. With all my strength, with all my pain, with all my hatred and revenge, the first blow laid the monster to the ground. Again and again I struck its head. Over and over I smashed its skull till it was nothing but the bloody pulp of brain and bones. Venting with nothing more to live for, enveloped in a fire of burning pain, I struck repeatedly out of frustrated rage.

"I'll kill you!" I screamed at the madness of existence. "I'll destroy you!" I cursed the force responsible for it all. Dragging myself forward, hobbling along on a stump of a leg I ranted and raved abominations of disgust. Thrashing about, lashing out at every living thing, I rampaged my way through this incarnate horror. I didn't care anymore. I didn't care about anything, for in an instant I saw the monstrous evil of life—the demonic nightmare of existence. It was all a hideous game. A horrifying dream. An absurd joke at my own expense. They were playing with me. Toying with me for their own amusement. Pulling my strings like a puppet and a fool. I wouldn't take it any longer. I'd strike back. I'd revolt and destroy their world. Drag them down into the pit of my own hell. Make them pay for what they've done to me.

"I'll kill you!" my voice echoed horribly through the world. Lashing about I taunted them to engage, challenging and demanding that they confront me now. It would be the end, but I didn't care. For nothing mattered but my own revenge. I'd destroy them all. I'd destroy everything. Ravaging the world. Slashing my way through the undergrowth. Smashing anything which got in my way. It was a living nightmare they wanted me to accept, and I was tearing it apart before their eyes, tearing existence into tiny shreds.

Then suddenly the horror converged. Without warning I was engulfed in a swirling mass of fur and flesh. Demons of all shapes and sizes were pouncing upon me and ripping my skin, tearing away at my arms and leg, biting and clawing my face and neck. Burning! Searing! Agonizing pain! Screaming in torment! Thrashing about to knock them away! Everyone was against me! The entire universe was my foe!

"Iris!" I cried out for mercy. But nothing changed. I was alone to face my own horrible destiny. Isolated within my own nightmare hell. "I'll kill you all !-!-!" I screamed from the depths of my soul. And suddenly I was lashing out in blind fury, taking the offense because I was offended. Rending and gashing with each ounce of strength. But it was too much for me. I was being overwhelmed. Choking! Smothering!

I was coughing up blood! Gasping for air! Struggling vainly for room to breathe! I was dying! It was finally over. The nightmare of my life was finally ending.

But it wasn't ending. It was just beginning. One, two, three—ready, set, go! We were on our way, across the configuration of a square, Stickman, Duckling, myself, and more, zigzagging back and forth relaying a pen for a baton. Hurry-hurry-hurry! Back and forth—back and forth. The pen was the instrument describing our course. But the pen was empty: it left no mark. And we reached the bottom of the square and dropped off. Duckling first, his awkward limbs flailing in the void. Stickman next, clattering to no avail. Myself, off the Structural corridor. There was a thump!

Her body lay passive as I stabbed it again and again, lashing that bitch until the covering actually tore, releasing a cloud of furry stuffing with each enraged blow. I smashed her head over and over, breaking the hard skull only to find that it was empty. "Bang!—Bang!" I shouted. "Bang! Bang!—Bang! Bang!" And they were falling about me, dropping to their knees and lying prostrate for the feast. Roast Duckling smothered in orange sauce. Tender frog legs. Fried caterpillars. Crunchy Stickmen. All prepared for my immediate enjoyment. And I did enjoy it. I ate until I threw up. And then, like a dog, I ate my own throw-up. And I ejaculated, and felt good . . . and then I cried . . .

"Iris!" I called out over and over. And I began beating myself with both fists. But no one was there. No one would come. She was only a construct of my mind. I began flailing my head against the ground. Over and over in order to smash that shell. It was my mind!—my mind!—I had to destroy. I had to destroy my consciousness in order to destroy thought. I had to destroy my mind in order to die for good.

I was smashing myself, crushing my bones and face to a pulp, cracking that skull until it eventually burst. Yet there was nothing there, nothing but an emptiness which could not die. I was floating. Drifting. Merging with the void. Fading into the subliminal abyss. Nothing existed in the oblivion of death—nothing but the lingering darkness of my mind.

As I journeyed through the darkness I seemed to see a faint light in the distance. Was it imagination? Was it illusion? Painfully I crawled forward on hands and knees, bruised and sore by my strenuous movements. My nocturnal vision was apparently correct, for the brightness grew proportionally to the distance traveled.

Reaching the light, I looked down from a screened vent onto a large stage surrounded by darkness with a small table and light in the center. Upon the table was an unfinished book whose unbound pages lay scattered in disarray. A sudden impulse made me pass through the vent, climb down to the stage and investigate the nature of this unfinished work. It seemed to be a textbook on mathematical expressions by some obscure professor. The pages were disordered. Some were perhaps missing. Thus the structure was violated. The meaning was out of context. However I did manage to capture the gist of the story. The story?

It was a geometric story about a mathematical progression into infinity. The plot was structured upon an algebraic proof. The subject, a mathematical symbol. The given, a variable with a value unknown. The form, by necessity, was the first person narrative. Thus it was as confusing as any subjective account. Nevertheless, picking a page at random, I proceeded to read it as it was.

> I was becoming bored. It was getting late and every moment I was growing older. And yet nothing was happening. The time had not yet come. I wanted to leave. I wanted to remove myself from these premises, but I simply could not respond. It was like a dream over which I had no control, for the story had no structure. Fragmented and distorted it seemed to lose all sense of meaning and purpose. It was simply there, as it was,

without excuse or justification, to be dealt with and interpreted as one saw fit.

I opened my eyes to the darkness of the theater. I was lying upon a stage surrounded by void, a totally square stage suspended in space. I was waiting as I had always waited. For there was nothing else to do, nothing but sleep, nothing but dream. But I couldn't sleep. I couldn't dream. I wasn't tired enough for sleep and dreams. Half-dazed I remained motionless in the confining darkness. I was too tired to move, and yet I was incapable of rest. I was delirious and nauseous, sickened by the pregnant emptiness of the void. I lay passive, gazing vacantly, watching and waiting as the dark figure sat quietly reading a book. Or was he writing it? It appeared by his movements as though he were plotting out points on a four-dimensional map of space and time. But I doubted my vision. My line of sight was indirect. Lying sideways, gazing up through the darkness at the desk, I could barely distinguish the movements of his form. Regardless of his actions I held him responsible, rose from my stupor, and proceeded to my goal.

He was doing something. That's all I knew. But whatever it was I didn't like it. The abomination before him was a blasphemy against life. It was a weird hypothetical projection of existence onto space, a holographic image of reality incarnate. But it wasn't incarnate. It was simply projected thought—a swirling mass of malformed images and ideas. It was the force itself! The universe in its nakedness. The absolute reality embracing the world. And there it lay before my eyes—a nauseating whirlpool of imagery without form, a vortex of scattered consciousness spiraling into a void, spiraling down into the maw of nothingness—a focal point of intangible force and motion, a theoretical focus which doesn't exist, a dream which vanishes and yet has effect. Sounds. Voices. Visions. Scenes passing before my eyes. Then swallowed up in the insatiable abyss. It was for this that I had traveled so far. It was for this that I had come all these years to find—a vortex of deranged power and thought. It was because of this that the universe had being. This was the reason behind existence—a freak inversion of nothingness into existence, a warped disturbance in the current of the void. Perpetual motion. Eternal flux. A vacuum of consciousness extending infinitely into the depths. A movement ever-approximating but never reaching its goal. Drawing infinitely closer, approaching eternally, but never quite forming, never quite reaching the end. But I would take it to the end! I would initiate the leap.

The dark figure stood motionless silhouetted against the projection. He was there. He was in the way. And he was responsible. He was plotting points and reorganizing the form. He was actively participating within the process. In one hysterical moment I pounced upon his neck. Choking with all my strength and energy I was finally striking back for all the horror of existence. Stunned by the attack, the passive entity whirled forward, collapsing into the throbbing projection of life. Holding on till the end, I too was caught within the whirlpool, strangling as we plunged into its depths.

As we swirled through the cosmic eddy I saw the

world passing before me. I saw the pain and suffering, the senseless absurdity, the mock futility of billions of lives. Eating. Sleeping. Working. Mating. Day after day. Year after year. Century after century without meaningful change. It was a senseless cycle of needless repetition. A tragic mockery since the dawn of man. Over and over throughout history the same tiresome farce dragged on and on. One by one they came into existence. One by one they passed away. Living for a moment, then lost forever—a passing phantom that would soon be gone.

In a flash I saw the horror of it all. Conscious entities struggling for life, enduring and suffering, starving and dying. I saw the disease and sickness, the maimed and crippled, the wars and bloodshed which rampaged through time. Pain, anguish, death, and destruction, futile longing and hopeless despair. And it was all for nothing. It made no difference, for the same tragic farce went on and on. I saw time compressed before my eyes. The world was spinning. My mind was reeling. I saw the nightmare horror of the prehistoric world. Monstrous abominations ravaging the earth. Devouring each other in wanton savagery. Struggling and murdering for hundreds of millions of years, then fading into the distant past. It made no sense! Eons and eons of useless toil and suffering. A billion years of terrestrial life struggling and dying in cosmic proportions. Yet it was all in vain. For they were already past. Myriads of sentient life forms striving unknowingly toward dead-end extinction. It was the ultimate folly. The panorama of an entire world wiped out and extinguished like so much trash. The victims of a fanciful whim. Sacrifices to the primal power.

Scenes and images flooded my eyes. Sounds and voices flashed through my mind. The entire universe passed before me, throbbing and convulsing in agonizing forms. Life itself was mutating into grotesqueness, mushrooming like a disease beyond control. I could see the universe as it was, raw and naked. Sentient beings devoured alive in slow, tormenting death. Helpless, innocent creatures torn apart by the process of insatiable life. I could hear the suffering that existed since the dawn of time. The crying. The screaming. The wailing. The shrieking. I could see the pain and anguish. The murder and brutality. The torturous death-throes of countless lives.

"I'll kill you!" I screamed. Strangling and choking with all my might I was destroying the dark figure once and for all. It was working. He was finally dying. The world transformed before my eyes. Strange visions reeled before my mind. I saw the butterflies in their ethereal splendor dancing about from flower to flower—then suddenly, crumpled and motionless, frozen to death with the first autumnal frost or snow. It was absurd! It was insane! Zeta! Zeta!! Zeta!!! I saw it all before my eyes. The Professor was wrong. There was no object. There was no goal. There was no motion but apparent motion. The axioms were all wrong. Zero point nine nine nine extended equals one. It was impossible, but it was true. I saw the world as it really was—a little, toy ball spinning off through space. It was Stickman's world surrounded by nothingness, an endless circle with nowhere to go. The mind-shattering images rolled on and on. My life flashed past me. I saw the foolishness and wasted energy. The pointless dreams and meaning-less goals. I saw the appalling vision of the Structure, realizing at once what its sight entailed. My entire journey amounted to nothing, for in the end I simply returned to the start. There was no region east or west, for it was all a circle, an endless cycle, a mean-ingless world without beginning or end. There was no goal, for the farther west you traveled, the more east it became. And the farthest you could go was to remain motionless in place.

We were spiraling, tumbling, accelerating through the world. Sucked headlong into the very core of be-ing. I could hear noise and confusion. Moans and screams. Billions of dreamers crying out in anguish, for life itself was only a dream. It was a bitter awak-ening. The senseless nightmare had finally ended. Existence itself would be no more. Sobbing over the horror of a lifelong madness, they could scarcely be-lieve that it was true. How could they have been deceived for so long? How could they possibly have accepted it as true? The world was collapsing before their eyes. Their loves, their joys, their hopes, their dreams—everything they lived for was no longer real.

* * * * *

Once more my weary eyes opened to the world. With great effort I saw what had to be seen. Lying motionless upon a hilltop I gazed vacantly over the deserted ruins of the Structure. I saw life as it really was: a make-believe Structure of endless dreams—a toy dollhouse that could only be closed up and put away. I raised myself upon the grassy slope. Looking over to Katon, whose eyes were half closing, I asked if we had won. A faint, sad smile crossed his face, then slowly disappeared.

The dream was over. The Revolution was a necessary tragedy. People stood in silence stunned and in shock. The sun was setting behind the western mountains, spreading golden light upon the world, offering its last rays of life and hope to weary dreamers who were again half asleep.

The cold, autumn breeze sent chills down my back. With hands in pockets, I stood, towering above, watching as the sun faded beneath golden, glowing clouds, watching as the crowd dispersed with the cool, night air. The world grew dark. Cold and empty, I watched the people wander through the passages back into the Structure—to their next fictitious life and dream.

As I saw, at once, the destiny of existence, a sudden calm indifference held me motionless to the world. I stood passively upon the hillside, endlessly awaiting the passage of time, patiently watching through cold, vacant eyes—as though I were Katon—and all my world was simply past, for he and I were one.

TRANSPOSITION

Asleep—Awake—There was no difference. All the future goals complete. Nothing more to fill the hours. Nothing more but empty dreams that vanish in the distant past. And now the lifeless world dismembered— lifeless gloom of gray remains. Time relinquished vast illusions. Today, tomorrow, now or later—eternity is all the same.

Aimlessly wandering, I drift through the world. Void of purpose and soul, I no longer seek. Forgetful of all former dreams, indifferent to all future life, I die a thousand times too late. And in the end I don't complain. I let it pass before my eyes—the pain, the useless suffering, endurance of appointed roles.

I wander through an endless dream, specter in an empty scene where nothing more is being shown.

Epilogue:
TRANSMIGRATION
or
THE CHRYSALIS

THE OVERCAST SPREAD from the east, contrasting the sun in the western skies. The cold front caught us unprepared as it moved in with the wind. And the sun was setting: a weak, yellow light spreading impotently through the cold, autumn air, shining full upon us, yet unable to effect the slightest warmth.

Dazed, as if in a dream, he sat patiently awaiting my return. His childish innocence was vulnerable to the elements. I could have destroyed him where he sat. Anyone else would have done so without thought, but the image held fast, for it made no difference what I did and so I returned. He realized that I had spared him and thus he followed in my footsteps, knowing only that he was safe within my presence. I moved quickly, trying to outrun the storm which darkened the sky. Yet even in such danger I could not help wondering whether the sun would set before the overcast was complete. Really it was only a whim, but somehow I was unable to resist watching as the overcast spread toward the western mountains.

I glanced back and noticed him lagging behind. His small, weak legs stepped delicately over the ground, pausing here and there, hesitant with each step. He became frantic as my distance grew, and he scrambled to keep me in sight. I too panicked on realizing I had lost my way, for the storm forecasted certain death to those caught unprepared. I was uncertain of the direction, but all that mattered was to keep moving. And so I ran through the woods in search of shelter, constantly aware of the impending storm and the increasing darkness compounded by the thick cover of overhanging trees.

Eventually I broke through into a small, provincial valley and discovered a mountain cottage high upon the hillside. It captured the dying light, reflecting yellow in the sunset, inviting everyone with its radiant warmth. Strangely I knew I had been there before. Some secret dream compelled me there, and with each step up the slope I felt closer to my destiny.

I climbed until I was out of breath. I looked back and was surprised to find him still following— his strained effort all for my presence, for in this hostile environment I was the only one he trusted, the only one with whom he could identify. I continued trudging up the steep slope, bracing and pulling myself with rocks and saplings. I could barely move, but each time I glanced back he was drawing nearer. His ability to climb was amazing. He scampered up the hill and was almost upon me when I reached the top, moving over the ridge and out into a pastoral meadow.

The overcast was complete. I would never know whether the sun had set. The dark, gray world seemed transformed and eternal. A calm sadness hung over the air—prelude to the silent storm. Deep inside I knew what I was looking for, but as I walked toward the house a vague suspicion lurked within its trans-formation. The sunset house seen from the valley was incompatible with this common, gray evening, middle-class home. Yet my hope continued. After all these years I had finally returned. I crossed the lawn and, gathering myself together, knocked firmly on the front door. I waited anxiously as footsteps approached from within, but something felt wrong. The door swung open and a strange lady stood facing me.

"Why did you knock?" she asked in a puzzled tone. "The door was open."

She picked up the newspaper off the porch and left me standing in the doorway, returning to her seat on the couch. I stood watching as a small boy and girl played with toys on the thick, red carpet. The dream was vague in essence, the reality too clear to be seen. Was the little girl playing with a dollhouse? Was the little boy playing with soldiers and aliens? Confusion held me helplessly in the midst of the ordinary. Slowly I withdrew, walking back around to the side street which cornered the house. Like a child, I sat down upon the curb in bewilderment. Thoughts and pictures flashed through my mind try-ing to drive me crazy, but I refused to be a passenger. Eventually I calmed to indifference, my mind suc-cumbing to a half-conscious state of shock.

* * * * *

Light flakes of snow drifted gently to the ground. The old man lay motionless in the gutter. He awoke as a flake settled on his eyelash, melted, and drizzled water onto his eyelid. He was cold, but there was nowhere to go, and even if there were it no longer made any difference. Moment after moment he lay huddled back against the curb. The desolate streets occasionally produced passers-by who hurried off as quickly as they came. From a nearby cafe two young couples with too much to drink came roaring and laughing onto the sidewalk. They mocked the old man in a language he could not understand, tossing him a coin as they went on their way. They did not care, and he did not want them to care, for he realized far too late that it didn't really matter. He could no longer feel the increasing cold. The numbness made him drowsy as a thin, white blanket formed over his body.

* * * * *

Approaching footsteps woke me from my dream. Glancing downhill, I watched a vaguely familiar person advance swiftly up the slope. A feeling of strength rekindled as he drew near, but the sense of an alien dream remained. For the situation was lost, and the most that I could hope for was comfort—a brief respite from the kaleidoscope of life.

"What happened?" he asked as he sat down upon the curb.

"She's not there," I said sadly. "They're all gone." He understood, for he had once been in my shoes, yet now he was no longer involved.

While we sat in silence the sky darkened even more, for even behind the overcast the effect could be felt as the sun pulled away from the edge of the world. He showed me an ancient manuscript or journal which somehow he had smuggled unnoticed up the hill.

"It's what we've been searching for," said a tired face that tried to smile.

There was no title or author, and when I opened the worm-eaten book I found myself at the end. Yet even upside-down I recognized the significance of the concluding lines. I turned the book over and, in the dim gray light, read slowly the haunting words which marked the end of the story.

No one knows me, for I am not real. I am an illusion that deceives the eyes. I am an illusion that distorts the mind. All who think they know me, know only an illusion, for the real me exists somewhere between zero and infinity.

He watched closely to observe my reaction. Closing the cover, I sat motionless as the void converged. No longer did it matter one way or another. No longer did I care whether it began once more.

"Bedtime!" called a woman's voice from the balcony porch. I glanced up to see the lady gazing down from above.

"Your mother's calling," said my companion, "you'd better go in."

"My mother?" I repeated. And now I was dumbfounded, but I was too tired and too sleepy to separate dreams from reality.

Gazing out past the horizon, lost in another world, my friend seemed unaware as I left him by the curb. I carried the ancient book across the yard and timidly entered the house, feeling unable to justify my presence in their home. The two children were still playing games on the rug, and now a man was sitting in a reclining chair reading a paper. I was surrounded by the unfamiliar and so I walked up the stairs and entered my room. I felt uneasily like a traveler in strange, public lodgings. Something was wrong. Something was missing. Bewildered and in a daze I sat down at a small table and once again opened the book. The illustration on the front-piece was of a Stickman pulling and tearing at his hair. The end-piece was of a frog dancing with a goddess. An excerpt at random began like this:

> The worst deception is that of oneself. And the worst enslavement is that of the mind. Few can conceive this world of men who deceive and enslave only themselves. But each slave has a key to freedom. The key is his to do as he will.

Though still confused, I seemed to have gained a vague understanding of my situation. I flipped carefully through the pages of the manuscript, yellow from age, brown and crackly along the edges as if scorched by fire. At the top of a page I glanced past the words, **BEAUTIFUL ILLUSIONS**, in bold type. I flipped back to the page and read:

> Emptiness and despair, then suddenly a warmth and joy. Sad smile, happy smile with tear-clouded eyes, forced to love with sorrow.

She sees the sunset on the meadow pond. The duck paddles by. The frog plops in. And a face looks down to the sky. See the world so still as the butterfly sleeps with a caterpillar dream. Such a pond, so alert as nothing beholds.

She walks on with a peaceful air. No thoughts, no words, just empty dreams. An image of a happy face—transcendent smile, surreally there. Look in her gaze. What can you see? A pond, a frog, the autumn moon.

She passes by and glances up. "Hello," we smile and walk away. Then suddenly, as I drift asleep, "Goodbye," a soft voice fades away. Turn around! No, just keep walking. Look back for her when you know she's gone. And feign surprise. "Too late!" I cry. Forgotten dream, forever lost. Yet feelings linger through the day, soft voices fading, calm understanding. What did she say? "Frogs sing and dance?" Tomorrow remains my yesterday.

Completion of the circle—the tragedy of understanding. Sadly dreaming, gazing over the pages of the chapter, I discovered a strange entry. The words enticed and lured me away, reminiscent of a lost dream of another world:

Enthralled by its beauty and calm innocence, he gazed into the soft, glowing light. From within its depth emerged thin, delicate crystals, glittering shades of blue and green, sparkling like a cavern of diamonds and gems. The crystal lights struck him with awe and wonder, filling him with a warmth and comfort he could not explain.

I closed my eyes and turned away. I had no desire to read any further. Pretending to be asleep I leaned back with closed eyes, but it was of no use, for I continually returned to the crystalline light, the calm gentle light that glowed within the void. The light played upon my soul, laughing and dancing, smiling and soothing, but I was afraid! Fear of its strangeness gave me cold, trembling hands. Fear of its certainty gave me nervous, hesitant steps that finally retreated into the past. But I was tired of imagination! For once I would be responsible for my reality. I opened my eyes and searched for the title, BEAUTFUL ILLUSIONS. Page by page I thumbed through the book, but it was gone. It had vanished like a dream, a dream I tried desperately to recall, but which had passed beyond reach. I proceeded casually through the random pages until I chanced upon a story:

He opened his eyes to the darkness of the room. Glancing at the clock he saw it was three in the morning. When would it end? When could he ever rest? He dressed and walked out into the cold, black silence. The arctic air enveloped him in a mist. Instantly his body chilled. Within moments pain struck his fingers and ears. He hated it! Where was it leading him? He was tired and sleepy. He longed to be back in bed. He listened to the dead silence, the empty stillness of a frozen, stagnant world. Unconcerned and unaware, the world slept peacefully through the night. He was disillusioned and about to turn back when suddenly his feet reached the snowy path. The light, powdered snow crunched under his boots, echoing footsteps through the tall, pine trees. The sound in the soundless, the heartbeat of perfection, filled his body with courage and strength. The footsteps resounded through the hidden world like the regimental march of a one-man army. Half asleep, dazed by the illusion of life, his soul wandered back and lingered in the bright, crystal cavern of his dream.

With that I walked out into the cold, black silence and set the ancient manuscript ablaze. . . . For each man must write his own book. . . . Each man must dream his own dream. . . .

www.ingramcontent.com/pod-product-compliance
Lightning Source LLC
Chambersburg PA
CBHW060636260626
47161CB00008B/2907